Foxtrot in Freshby

Awen Thornber

CROOKED
CAT

Copyright © 2017 by Awen Thornber
Artwork: goonwrite.com
Editor: Sue Barnard
All rights reserved.

No part of this book may be used or reproduced in any manner whatsoever without written permission of the author or Crooked Cat Books except for brief quotations used for promotion or in reviews. This is a work of fiction. Names, characters, and incidents are used fictitiously.

First Crooked Love Cats Edition, Crooked Cat, 2017

Discover us online:
www.crookedcatbooks.com

Join us on facebook:
www.facebook.com/crookedcat

Tweet a photo of yourself holding this book to **@crookedcatbooks** and something nice will happen.

*For my parents,
Marjorie and Alan Thornber,
who always believed
I'd be a published author.*

About the Author

Formerly a textile artist and design consultant for a craft company, Awen Thornber produced craft projects and articles for magazines, and had a regular craft column in Northern Life magazine. She is always looking for inspiration to spark her creative mind and currently devotes her time to writing novels. Born and bred in Lancashire, Awen also loves walking, painting, ballroom and ballet dancing.

Acknowledgements

I would like to thank Anne, who has been my brainstorming friend, encouraging and nagging me for over fifteen years to keep writing even when life got in the way. You have waited patiently for me to finish a novel and submit it to a publisher. I hope you will enjoy reading it.

To Paula and Carol my author friends. Who would have thought a casual chat on FaceBook would result in us meeting up regularly the last three years, to talk about writing and to support each other? A special mention to Paula for her invaluable advice and editing prior to my submitting to Crooked Cat.

I want to thank: my husband, Peter, and my children Gill and Phillip for believing in me; also Maureen of McDonald Dance Academy for teaching me to dance and answering my hypothetical questions about the dance competition.

Finally, but importantly, a huge thank you to Laurence, Stephanie, Sue and the whole Crooked Cat Author community for their invaluable advice and support.

Foxtrot in Freshby

Chapter One

Gina hurled the Christmas ornament at the wall.

It was the first she and Tony had bought together.

The sound of the glass shattering on impact, and the sight of the coloured shards that were once a snowy village scene flying through the air to rain down on her oak floor, was surprisingly satisfying.

She looked around the room for some other object on which to vent her anger, and her glance reached the twinkling tree in the corner of the bay window.

"Don't look so smug," she muttered. "You're next. Christmas is officially over, and you're going in the loft."

Without the gentle touch she had used to decorate the tree three weeks previously, she pulled and tugged at the ornaments.

The sound of banging on the glass at her side made her jump. She looked around to see Tony, standing by the window nearest to the front door, holding his key in front of him. He glared at her.

"Let me in. You've put the lock on!"

She shook her head.

"Don't play games, Gina. Open the bloody door. It's pouring down out here."

For the first time, she realised the rustling she'd heard in the background had been the sound of rain pattering against the window.

"Just open the bloody door!"

She automatically tied her belt tighter and held together the collar of her fleecy dressing gown as she reached up to open a window.

"What do you want?"

"I'll tell you what I don't want. I don't want to stand here in the sodding rain, holding a bloody conversation, through a bloody window."

"You are n*ot* coming in. I have nothing to say to you. You can say what you came to say, here and *now*, and then leave your key and go."

Tony pulled his collar up and looked around to see if anyone was about in the road. So what, Gina thought, if he was uncomfortable having a conversation through the window? He should have thought of that before coming to the house.

"We need to talk about it, Gina. You can't just give up everything we had together."

"*Me* give it up? *You* obviously didn't care a toss about everything we had, whatever that was. You certainly didn't care about me, just yourself."

"I was drunk. It was a moment of…"

"After an hour? You had two beers at the most. Since when have you been drunk on two beers? I'm not arguing with you. Pass me your keys and sod off."

He tightened his fist around the key.

She still had hold of her dressing gown, which was a good thing as her chest was rising and falling at an alarming rate. She bit her cheek. She was tired through lack of sleep, and if she didn't hold back, she would start screaming at him, and lose all her self-control.

"For God's sake, Tony, just get lost. You obviously don't give a shit about me. It's been more than seven hours since I left the party, on my own, and now you have the cheek to turn up here accusing *me* of giving up everything we had! Leave me alone. Give me the keys, or don't give me them and I'll change the locks. Either way, you won't set foot in this house again!"

"Oh, for pity's sake!" He let out a frustrated huff. "Okay, if you are going to persist with that idiot attitude, Gina, then just let me in, so I can get some of my things. I need clean clothes for work tomorrow."

"You don't need to come in for your things. I bagged them

up when I got home last night. They're all waiting for you by the bins."

"You bitch!" He ran to the side of the house and shouted, "Surely you haven't put my Jaeger suits and expensive shoes in the bags?"

She looked at the rain bouncing off the drive, raised herself up on to her toes, and shouted through the window.

"Everything! Everything you own! All in black bin bags! Oh yeah, they may be a bit wet! I can't remember if I tied the bags properly."

Last night, she'd been in no fit state to think carefully. It had been a painful walk home from the party, both emotionally and in her new kitten-heeled shoes. Her first rational thought had been to strip out of her wet clothes, and put on her snuggly warm lounge pants, cami, and dressing gown.

Watching Tony rescue the bags, she was thankful that somehow she had thought clearly enough to use the anger that burnt in her on the cold, lonely walk home to remove any trace of him from her house and life.

She smirked as she reached up to push the window latch down, and spied a movement by the hedge. Tony must have spotted it too, because he put two fingers up at her neighbour, Mrs Renwick, as he loaded the first batch of dripping bin bags into his car.

Moving away from the bay window gave her a chance to breathe properly, and steady her shaking hands. She shivered, realising how cold she was after standing in her unheated house under an open window, and ran upstairs to change into her jeans and jumper. Not wanting to give the impression that she cared, she deliberately kept away from the window, but heard Tony drive off.

Dressed, and with the heating turned up, she went downstairs again to continue stripping the tree.

She stopped as she cradled an angel in her hand. The wings were battered and the face scratched by years of being unpacked and repacked for the Christmas tree, but she was special. Her gran had given her the angel as part of her eighteenth birthday gifts. At the time it meant more than the cheque for driving lessons and the new coat that were given with it. It was the first ornament her gran and grandad had bought together as a newly-married couple. They were on a rare day trip together in the Lake District and spotted the angel in a small workshop run by a Dutch couple. The angel wore clogs and had, at one time displayed a small blue and white biblical scene painted on her dress, although this had worn off over the years and was now looking more like blue freckles or skin patches.

Before wrapping the angel in tissue paper, which she pulled out of a drawer in gran's old cabinet, she stroked it gently and held it to her lips. No matter how tatty the angel became, Gina would always treasure her.

She pulled off a few more ornaments, including the baby Jesus from Harrods. Her anger flared again at the memories.

"You lied!" she shouted at the small figure. "Lied!" And flung it at the wall. Somehow, the thought of baby Jesus being in league with Tony, yet all the while keeping a serene expression, riled her more than Tony had. The body fell first, followed by the head. The rest of the ornaments followed, hurled at the wall to join in the mess of broken glass and ceramic.

Guilt stabbed her at the religious implications of destroying the baby Jesus so violently, and she wondered if the heavens would hold it against her, until she remembered that this was probably the biggest betrayal of them all.

Her mind replayed the days in London she had spent with Lucy. Tony had paid for them to stay at a hotel and bought them tickets for Michael Bublé at the Hammersmith Apollo. Gina was on a salsa course, and Lucy had just split from yet another boyfriend.

She chewed her lip as she pictured Lucy turning up late at the theatre, looking flustered, her hair untidy, and muttering an excuse about falling asleep in the room and waking up too late to shower. Lucy had been keen to shop till she dropped, so what was she doing sleeping in the afternoon? Then there had been the London train ticket Tony had left in his shirt pocket. When she questioned him he said it had been a last-minute meeting, and as he was staying the opposite end of London to them, there was no point letting her know he was there. He'd bought the innocent-looking baby Jesus from Harrods on his way back to the train. Maybe it was fitting that, unusually, he'd picked it on his own. Especially when, looking back, she suspected he'd been responsible for Lucy's untidy hair and late arrival.

"Bastard!"

She struggled to untangle an overly fat Santa from a branch. A gift from Lucy during *that* trip. Her eyes smarted and she blinked hard. A single tear escaped, making a run for freedom down her cheek.

"I really don't care," she told the fat Santa as she tugged and pulled again. "They deserve each other." Then, throwing the tree to the floor, like a black belt going for the submission, she gave an anguished cry of "BITCH!"

She left the tree on the floor and went into the kitchen to calm herself with a mug of coffee. On her way she stared at herself in the hall mirror.

"You look a mess."

She ran a hand through her hair and shook the ends to separate the tangles. It didn't make her look any better, but she gained some comfort from the action. Her eyes stared back at her in the mirror, but she didn't recognise them. They were veiled, unreadable, defensive. She sighed. She knew she could be strong enough to bounce back; she had survived her parents' emigration, followed by their divorce. She'd struggled through the months after her gran's death, but her career was up and running within that year.

"Get over it," she said sternly to the mirror. A blank expression faced her. She turned away. "Get over it," she said softly to herself, as she went into the kitchen to switch the kettle on.

She carried the mug of coffee into the lounge, along with a roll of sturdy bin bags. After taking the tree apart she stuffed it into one of the bags, gathered up the lights and the fragments of the ornaments into another, and took them out to the bin.

Fifteen minutes later, as she sat in the bath and soaped her legs, she thought about her gran again.

"Gran," she whispered, "what do I do now?"

Tony had paid her a rent of sorts, which helped with the bills, and she'd had use of his car. It had worked well.

At least she hadn't been foolish enough to give him a half-share in the house, which had been her inheritance from her gran. He'd been happy with the arrangement they made.

She groaned. She needed to find some other way to make enough money to keep running the house on her own.

When Gran was a young married woman, she'd rented a dance hall and given lessons in drama and performing arts. The income from it had depended on people turning up, and in times of hardship or bad weather the events and classes were poorly attended. Despite all that, Gina never saw Gran defeated or scruffy, even around the house, and she always had a smile for people.

She'd probably inherited her dance genes from Gran, and hopefully an ounce or two of her determination. Her first job as a junior dance teacher had been in a school run by a former pupil of Gran's, and that experience saw her present career, as a freelance dance teacher, grow from strength to strength. As she lay back to soak in the hot bath, she realised just how much she had to thank her gran for, so she blew a kiss to the heavens, and closed her eyes.

The idea came to her whilst she was towelling her hair dry. She mulled it over in her mind, then smiled. Maybe, just maybe, the plan could work.

After wrapping the bath sheet around her body, she went down the stairs and stood in the doorway of her lounge.

It was a large room, and now that Tony had gone she would hardly use it. The kitchen and dining room would be much cosier and warmer. She looked around for a few more minutes, before pushing the sofa, chairs, coffee table, side tables and lamps, to the edges.

When she'd moved the last obstacle, she surveyed the room again. A chuckle escaped her lips. It resembled a doctor's waiting room! She stood in the centre and turned around slowly, clockwise. Would it be big enough? It would do. She could do it, she was sure of it.

To prove to herself there was enough space, she picked a sequence from the dance that would cover a larger area of floor than most, and began to try it out.

After making a box step to the side and back again, while humming a tune, she took three steps backwards, and then three more. Stepping to the side again she used sixteen steps to turn full circle. She strode out towards the wall, and back in the opposite direction to the bay window.

Taking a deep breath, she leant against the doorway once more.

"It could work." The excitement welled up in her chest and escaped from her throat in a croaky squeal. "Yes! This *will* work!"

Chapter Two

Gina gathered up all the sheets of paper and forms on the kitchen table, shuffled them into a neat pile, and breathed a sigh of relief.

With the legal side of the arrangements completed, the council informed and insurance in place, all she had to do now was advertise.

She jotted down a few sentences until she was happy with the detail, and phoned the *Freshby Times*.

"Ooh, sounds like fun," said the voice on the other end. "Do I need to bring a partner?"

"Not at all. I can partner you, or there may be an odd number in the class. Do you think I should add *'No partner required*'?"

They agreed it might be worth the extra cost to the advert, so she paid with her credit card and took the details of her new dance student.

"See you soon, Darren. Make sure you wear comfortable shoes but not trainers. They're too bulky, and tennis shoes or rubber-soled shoes may stick to the floor rather than glide. Other than that, just bring yourself."

She sat back and smiled. Hopefully recruiting a new student within minutes of setting up on her own was a sign of even better things to come. She would still carry on teaching dance freelance until she had enough to hire her own studio, but in the meantime using her lounge for a few nights a week would suffice.

Although it was difficult and strenuous work to move all the furniture out of the room, the bigger problem was deciding where to put it all. It didn't look a lot in the large lounge, but when she tried to squeeze it in the dining room and hallway there was far too much.

It might fit into the spare bedroom, as it was sparsely furnished with only a bed and bedside cabinet, but how was she going to move all the heavy cabinets upstairs?

She moved aside one of the cabinets to open the drawer in the hall table, then flicked through her phone book for the number of *The Local Shop* and dialled.

"Hi Shelley. I was hoping to speak to Paul: is he around? I wondered if he and one of his friends would do me a favour? I'll give them a few pounds each."

"He's left, Gina. He didn't want to work the long hours, he kept letting me down, so just me and Geoff here now. I can't be bothered with the hassle of advertising, interviewing and sorting out new staff. What's your problem? Can Geoff help?"

"I don't want to drag him away from the shop, but I need some assistance with moving furniture."

She explained her plan to Shelley, and heard her asking Geoff if he fancied a break while they had a lull in customers. "That's fine, Gina. He likes any excuse for a change from standing behind the counter, with only shelves to look at. He's grabbing his coat and he'll be around in two ticks."

"Great, thanks. I owe you."

"Not at all. You've helped us out before, so this makes us even now. Good luck with your new venture."

Maybe she was being somewhat optimistic, thinking they could lift the heavy furniture up the stairs between them, but she left her front door open for Geoff to let himself in. She was in the kitchen searching for some gloves to protect her hands and help her grip, when she heard a noise.

She returned to the hall to greet Geoff and blinked in surprise. "Oh!"

"Hi Gina. I've brought Chris to help me. He was loitering in the shop so I suggested he could make himself useful. Gina Pendleton, meet Chris Jackson. Chris, meet Gina."

She held her hand out to shake Chris's, and wondered why his face seemed familiar.

At over six feet tall, attractive in a fresh-faced, boyish kind of way, with stunning blue eyes – the sort she wanted to stare into – she knew she wasn't mistaken in thinking their paths had crossed at some point. She realised she still had a grip on his hand as she searched his face for a clue about where they'd met. If he lived in Freshby, perhaps they'd passed each other in the town centre.

"Sorry, but, have we met before?"

"Not met, exactly." He paused. "I was at the same Boxing Day party, and I was going to offer you a drink, but you shot past me and left early before I was able to speak to you."

"Ah!" She vaguely remembered a hesitant guy standing by the door as she rushed away from the party. "I see. Sorry."

"No problem. How can we help?"

Glad to change the subject, she explained her plan and where she needed the furniture moving.

"Right," said Geoff. "Put the kettle on, love, and we'll get to it. Won't take us long."

Geoff was right. Between them, the men manoeuvred the cabinets, display case and small armchair upstairs. They moved the two sofas and coffee table into the area just off the kitchen that she still called the dining room, despite the absence of the dividing wall that used to separate it from the kitchen. They moved the dining furniture in to the empty front room.

As she watched them carrying a cabinet up the stairs, she couldn't help but admire Chris's physique. He was slim with broad shoulders and a very neat bum, accentuated by his close-fitting, cotton canvas jeans. Much more attractive than Geoff's baggy denim ones, pulled in by a belt under his pot belly.

Within half an hour they joined her for coffee and biscuits in the kitchen. She noted Chris's thick, tousled head of hair (another contrast from Geoff's thin and fine hair), and she resisted the urge to reach out and run her fingers through it. He was in good shape. Maybe he went to the gym regularly.

"Thank you so much for helping. I couldn't have managed it on my own."

"I hope you make a success of it, Gina," Geoff said. "There's already a very successful dance school in Freshby, so you may find it hard to recruit students, unless you are offering something different."

"I don't think they offer Argentine tango classes, which is what I intend to run. I can't teach some of the ballroom dances such as quickstep and foxtrot because the room isn't big enough. Thankfully I do have a decent hard-wearing wooden floor, or I couldn't have considered setting up classes from home at all. I don't have the money to hire a hall."

"I thought you were happy being employed by the dance school. Self-employment may not earn you enough to live off."

"I'll still teach my freelance classes at the Wigan dance school, Geoff." She sighed. "The only problem is that I don't have the use of a car now. I've looked into trains to Wigan and the journey will take me an hour and a half each way. In the daytime it's possible, but evenings will be difficult, and the price of the train fare will eat into my wages. I need to try and make a go of teaching here."

"Ah, yes. Tony's car. I forgot you would be car-less. Well, I admire your spirit, girl. No use moping around and letting life get to you. I wish you luck. You deserve it for sheer determination." He nudged Chris. "We ought to go now. Thanks for the coffee, but if I don't park my backside behind the counter again soon, I'll get the silent treatment from Shelley. Come on, Chris."

Chris hadn't said a word during their coffee and biscuits. He'd spent the duration of their chat looking down and studying his coffee mug, as if avoiding eye contact, silently tapping the mug handle with his finger. Was he wishing he'd gone as soon as the furniture had been moved?

He paused at the front door and the memory shot into her mind of his expression as she'd rushed past him at the party. Almost as if he wanted to say something but wasn't sure what or how to say it. She offered her hand.

"Bye, Chris. Thanks for coming with Geoff to help. I appreciate it."

He shook her hand. "You're welcome." After a slight hesitation and a glance around at Geoff, he turned away and the two men walked down the path.

She closed the door and leaned against it. What was that all about?

Had Chris been weighing her up, judging her whilst she'd been talking to Geoff? Or was he genuinely awkward about being dragged to the house of an emotionally unstable female? How much did he know about her exit from the party? She'd only told Shelley she'd split up with Tony and was reorganising her career.

A slight quiver ran through her as she wondered what he'd been about to say as she slipped past him that night. Maybe she was reading too much into it. Perhaps he was shy, or just one of those people who can't leave without hovering at a door for too long.

With the two men gone, her house seemed too quiet and her thoughts taunted her. So in an effort to keep busy, she designed some flyers on the computer. Pleased with the result, she planned to distribute them to local shops and gyms. The rest of the afternoon was spent going through her music collection and compiling a selection of songs suitable for Argentine tango on her iPod. She moved her docking station into the lounge and set it up on the loose-leaf dining table, which was pushed against the wall next to the door.

The dining chairs were also against the wall next to the table, for students wanting to take a break from dancing. The room appeared so much more spacious without all the original furniture, but it needed a few full-length mirrors to finish it off. She looked at her watch. The shops in the village would still be open, and she might find what she was looking for there.

Grabbing her coat from the hall stand she reached for her keys. Only when she picked them up did she remember that she no longer had the use of Tony's car. By the time she'd walked into the village the shops would be closing.

"Damn you, Tony Ward. Why wasn't I enough for you?" She stared at the car key in her hand. "And where the hell do I send this to? Lucy's? Your office?" She certainly didn't want to meet him to return the car key. Sending it to Lucy's would be the best option.

Clutching the keys so tightly in her hand that they bit into her palm, she fought back the tears gathering behind her eyes. She released her fingers to ease the pain her grip was causing, and her tears started to flow.

After fumbling with the key ring, she managed to separate the car key from her house keys, found an envelope in a cupboard, and left the car key inside it on the hall stand. It wasn't urgent. He still had his own car key, and she would decide what to do with this one later.

The tears trickled down her cheeks and round her nose, but letting them flow freely calmed her down. She brushed away the droplets from her chin, cupped her face into her hands and let her shoulders droop.

Being single didn't bother her. She wasn't even sure if she would miss Tony, once she dealt with the knot of pain in her chest and the queasy feelings in her stomach. When anyone had asked her, she told them theirs was a companionable relationship. She could have explained that they didn't need the fireworks and fanfares but were comfortable just being together, choosing to stay in, cuddle on the couch and watch a film or DVD. Their three years together had consisted of snatching short breaks during gaps in her work and his. They hadn't gone out on many date nights once he moved into her house, which had been his idea. "I stay here overnight so often," he'd said, "that I may as well move my things in, give up my flat and use my rent money to help you run this house."

The truth was, as she realised a few months down the line, he was paying her less than his rent had been, and he was still always short of cash. "I'll pay you back at the end of the month," had become his catchphrase.

Now, of course, there was Lucy.

Was that the reason they didn't need fireworks? Was it because he was experiencing the whole glorious light show elsewhere? If so, for how long?

"Enough!"

Deep thinking wasn't what she needed. In the kitchen she poured herself a large measure of gin and topped it up with a smaller measure of tonic.

"This is what I need."

She downed it quickly. The sudden rush of alcohol, coupled with the lack of food and her fragile emotions, made her feel warm and relaxed. She reached for the gin bottle, poured herself another drink, took the glass to the sofa and opened her laptop.

"Right, Google! Large cheap mirror, low delivery charges, quick delivery."

She awoke a few hours later, unfolded her legs slowly and rubbed them to relieve the pins and needles in her feet and calves. Even doing that was difficult, since one arm was numb and limp from lying on it against the hard sofa side. She waited for the life to come back gradually and painfully into her limbs, and toyed with the alternatives of either going to bed, or carrying on her fruitless search for suitable mirrors.

A glance at the clock told her it was half past seven. Useless going to bed now, she would be wide awake by three in the morning. Not a good idea, better to persevere with Google and maybe catch a film on TV or something else to waste the rest of the evening.

She made herself some tea and toast, switched on the TV, and watched a reality-type game show. The contestant's friends had chosen a blind date for her from a choice of C-list celebrities, and the cameras followed them everywhere for a week, interviewing them and generally getting in the way.

Despite all her mixed feelings, Gina couldn't help but laugh. The girl had overdone the fake tan, making her skin orange-toned, and her false eyelashes could have doubled as road sweepers. The guy was playing to the cameras with his boyish smile.

Her heart gave a little jump. Tony had a smile like that, the kind that made you want to smile with him. His smile was what had attracted her to him when they first met. He smiled, she melted. No doubt it attracted other girls too.

She bit into her toast and concentrated on the programme.

Now the couple were trying to outdo each other, talking only about themselves and not showing any real interest in the other person. The girl constantly delved in her handbag for make-up, phone, and perfume, whilst the man kept looking around to make sure people were watching him. On Day Three, the girl noticed his car had a scent that was neither his aftershave nor her perfume. She harped on about there being another woman's perfume. The guy denied it, but a forgotten memory jerked in Gina's mind.

She rushed upstairs to her bedroom and sniffed the duvet and pillows.

On several occasions, after she'd been teaching in the evening, she'd remarked on the vanilla fragrance in their bedroom. Tony had pointed to the candles on the hearth and mantelpiece in the lounge, suggesting the smell had wafted upstairs.

It had seemed a perfectly rational explanation at the time, but now she suspected the smell had been the vanilla base of the celebrity perfume Lucy always doused herself in.

She sniffed again, certain she hadn't mistaken the faint sweet, warm and woody fragrant tones clinging to Tony's pillow.

With a grunt of anger, she tore the covers off the bed and replaced them with a bed set scented by the fresh jasmine and green tea aroma of washing pearls.

Worn out with both her emotional reaction as well as the effort of stripping and remaking the bed, she lay down on top of the duvet and closed her eyes.

A loud ringing sound woke her up. It took a while to distinguish the noise from the scene that had been playing out in her subconscious as she dozed. When she realised what the sound was, she sat bolt upright.

She ran down the stairs to open the door, but with eyes still blurry from waking up, she took a couple of seconds to register who was standing there.

"Chris?"

Chapter Three

"Sorry, it's a bit late." Chris said. "I should have left it until tomorrow, but I wasn't sure if you would be in then. I saw the light on and it seemed a good idea to catch you now." He stopped his rush of words and looked down at his feet. "Sorry, I woke you up, didn't I?"

She automatically put her hand up to her hair to run her palm down the back of her head. Realising her hair wasn't going to lie flat easily, she tried to try finger-comb it instead.

Chris tried not to smile but failed, and the end of his lip curled up on one side. That one small movement was endearing and infectious. She smiled back and gave up on trying to straighten her messy hair, letting her hand drop to her side.

"I must have dozed off. I hadn't gone to bed." Why did she always feel the need to explain herself? Another habit she had developed from living with Tony. A simple yes would have done.

Chris was now looking directly at her. His smile had gone, but his eyes were soft with a visible warmth. She lowered her defensive barrier, and wondered whether to ask him in or let him talk on the doorstep.

He cut into her thoughts.

"I know a party is probably the last thing you will want to go to in the – erm – circumstances." Once again, his feet gained his focus. "But I was wondering – hoping – that you might consider coming to a New Year's Ball with me. A week on Saturday – January the eleventh." He lifted his head and looked straight at her face, his eyes focussed on hers as if searching for a hint of – what? Compassion? Interest? Resignation?

She wasn't ready for socialising. Why had she let her guard down? Panic crept in, and visions of rabbits caught in headlights flashed in front of her. She understood their fear.

"No! Don't worry. I didn't mean as a girlfriend." He put his hand out as if to touch her, but let it stay in the air between them, like a priest giving a blessing. "Oh God, I'm useless at this. I thought, with you teaching dance, that you could be my partner. To dance with, I mean. I wasn't asking for more. I know it's probably not the right time, but I already have the tickets." He paused, and when he spoke again it was less rushed. "I didn't want to go, but I was guilt-tripped into buying them." He shrugged before adding, "And I thought you might like to go to just dance, if you didn't have anything else planned, you know, with you being on your own now."

There, it was out in the open. He had stated the obvious and she could almost see the words illuminated between them like a huge neon sign with arrow pointing down at her.

"You thought because I no longer have a boyfriend, that I don't have friends to hang out with either?"

"Not at all." His cheeks reddened, which made her feel guilty for embarrassing him. The poor guy was probably telling the truth, and hadn't thought past the fact that she liked ballroom dancing and he had tickets for a ball.

She gave him a wry smile. She'd probably regret it, but what the hell? She had nothing to lose.

"Can you dance?"

"Badly, but if you lead I can follow and pick it up." He raised his eyebrows in an unspoken question. Was he questioning his ability to pick up on her lead, or whether she had made her decision?

He spoke again, probably to fill the silence while she sorted the pros and cons battling inside her head.

"If you decide at any point in the evening that you don't want to be there, I'll call a taxi for you to go home." As he smiled at her, his mouth turned up at the corners and his gentle eyes looked into hers. "Saying yes doesn't mean you have to stay until the bitter end. I may even want to play Cinderella and escape before midnight myself." His smile vanished. "I didn't mean… That wasn't aimed at…"

Watching him trying to dig himself out of a hole by making a bigger hole, she made a decision.

"Okay, if you put it like that, why not? So long as I can leave if it all gets too much."

Relief spread across his face and he sighed, letting out a deep breath as if to release tension.

"Thank you, Gina. I'll book a taxi and pick you up at eight, if that's okay. No point in getting there too early. Did I mention it's a black tie and cocktail dress evening?"

"No, but it's not a problem."

There was an awkward moment when she wasn't sure whether to shake his hand, or follow through with a compliment, and he didn't seem to know either. Not being able to leave the doorstep was becoming a habit with him, and it made her hesitant too. She settled for giving him a smile that she hoped conveyed the message of *Lovely chat, but I need to go now*.

He still didn't leave. Instead he stepped forward.

Oh no, please don't let him lean in for a kiss!

"Erm…," He hesitated, obviously struggling to find the right words, and then pointed to her face. "You have, erm… something, erm…" He touched his own cheek. "Anyway I'll, erm… Yes, bye. See you on Saturday." With that, he made a quick retreat down the path.

She looked in the hall mirror and groaned. Butter and toast crumbs were glued to her cheek just above the corner of her lips.

Ugh! Typical. A heart-meltingly handsome guy asks her to a ball, and she has food smeared across her face. Delving into the pocket of her jeans, she pulled out a tissue and wiped her cheek clean. Was he only looking into her eyes to avoid staring at her cheek? Or had his eyes had connected with hers because he was interested in getting to know her? The thought surprised her, as did the tingling sensation which wove itself around her ribs.

She glanced at her watch. Half past nine. Who knocks at your door at that time, to casually ask you to a ball, if they're not interested in you? It wasn't as if she had other offers beating a path to her door. Once he looked at her, instead of at his feet, she could see the genuine warmth in his eyes and knew she wanted to see more.

Another part of her was still cursing Tony. If he had been faithful there wouldn't be strangers knocking at her door in the middle of the evening, taking pity on her with an offer to let her make a bad dancer look good.

She stomped up the stairs and gathered up the old bedding off the floor to wash. Still angry with Tony as she entered the kitchen, she ignored the washing machine, walked straight to the outside door, and threw the lot in the outdoor bin.

A movement at the side of the house caught her eye. She froze on the spot, watching for any sign of life. The night was still, and she was sure the whole road could hear her heart beating. It seemed to be bouncing noisily around in her chest, despite her holding her breath. When she was sure nobody was near the house, she turned to walk back to the kitchen.

A loud rustling sounded from the garden behind her, and she swung around to face whoever it might be, but again there was nothing, and no one. She stayed motionless for half a minute, before making a show of shrugging her shoulders as if she didn't care, and returning to the house.

Once inside the kitchen, her bravado disintegrated and her hands shook as she made several attempts to turn the key in the door. When she finally managed to lock it, she left the key in to stop any intruder being able to unlock the door from the outside.

Trembling, she closed the blinds and turned the light out, before rushing into the hall to make sure she'd locked and chained the front door.

Next, she crept back to the kitchen in the dark. All her senses alert for unusual noises, she peered through a narrow gap between the curtains. From that vantage point, she could see the garden, but not the side of the house.

After a few minutes, when she didn't spot anything unusual, her shaking had stopped although the beat of her heart still pounded loudly in her ears. The thought occurred to her that anyone watching the house might be waiting to see if any lights went on somewhere else inside. She needed to make it look as if she was moving around upstairs and not hiding in the kitchen. After running upstairs to put on the spare bedroom light, she returned to resume her surveillance near the curtains.

There had definitely been someone moving at the side of the house. If it was Tony wanting to collect something she hadn't bagged up, why didn't he just knock? But she was sure the only thing she still had was his car key. It certainly wouldn't be Lucy. She was too high-maintenance to chance getting her clothes soiled or her hair messed up. Plus Lucy was probably more worried about any revenge Gina would want to take out on her!

What about Chris? She knew nothing about him. He may know Geoff, but he was a stranger to her, he'd hardly said anything, he knew the layout of her house, and he'd knocked late at night. Why did she agree to go to the ball with him? Was he some sort of stalker?

Her legs were becoming numb from standing in the same position for so long. It was time she gave up. Whoever it was had long gone by now anyway. Maybe they guessed her intention to spy on the garden as soon as she entered the house.

After a thorough check of all the window and door locks and bolts, she snuggled under the duvet and turned out the light.

First thing in the morning, she would phone the locksmith to change all the locks. It was an expense she could do without, but Tony hadn't given the house keys back to her. For all she knew, he could have left them on the doorstep for her to find, but another person might have picked them up. Maybe Chris had rung the doorbell to check if she was in the house before breaking in, and only used the New Year's dance as an excuse when she opened the door.

Oh, this was silly! Why would Chris want to break in? If he was a shady character, Geoff wouldn't have brought him to the house. She was suspecting people without any evidence, when it was probably just kids messing around.

She tried to convince herself by using it as a mantra. "It's kids, and I'm making a drama out of nothing." She repeated it several times before giving up. The tiredness from earlier in the day had left her, and she lay awake on her back. Not wanting to read or move from under her warm duvet, she waited for sleep to wash over her.

The screech of an owl somewhere in the area pierced the quiet night air. As she lay there listening for it to cry out again, she caught the soft sound of tyres on tarmac. The car stopped, its engine still running, and then came the unmistakable click of a car door.

Right outside her house.

Throwing the covers back, she dived toward the window.

A saloon car, with no lights on, drove at a snail's pace past Mrs Renwick's house, heading toward the main road. Something odd about the car sent a warning shiver down her neck to her chest. Her breathing became shallow as she squinted at the registration plate, but it was impossible to see the number, even when the car passed a street light. What had she missed? As it crawled past the houses to the next street light, her stomach knotted.

The car didn't have a passenger, only a driver. Her mind struggled to make sense of all this. Obviously it was up to no good, since it was driving without lights. As it reached the main road, its lights came on and it sped off.

Something still niggled away at her. From what she could see of her front garden, there was nothing out of the ordinary, and she padded through to the back bedroom. Instinct told her to keep out of sight, so she pressed against the wall to watch from the side of the window.

Everything in her garden appeared normal, but she listened intently. Was that a sound? Trying to decipher what it was, she narrowed her eyes to focus on the direction she thought it came from. That particular area of the garden was crammed with overgrown shrubs and trees. She remembered the countless times she'd asked Tony to cut them back. She'd tried on the odd occasion to hack at them herself, but they were a mass of intertwined branches, and her five-foot-two-inch petite frame found it too difficult to make any sort of decent cuts into the tough old wood.

Hearing the sound again, she looked beyond the shrubs to the trees, and, through a gap in them, to the top of the garden wall. A pair of cats faced each other, partially hidden by branches and lit up by the security camera of the house behind hers.

Was she just being stupid, imagining things that weren't there? Her feet were cold because she hadn't stopped to put her slippers on, and the goosebumps on her body were more from the cold than from trepidation.

She gave the garden one more look, and went back to bed.

As soon as her head touched the pillow, she recalled the niggle she'd felt earlier and, with sudden clarity, knew what had troubled her.

The car had pulled up, the door closed, and immediately it drove off. The street lights only showed a driver. But there hadn't been enough time for the driver to get out of the car, get back in, and drive off. So there must have been a passenger.

She tensed. If the passenger had been dropped off at one of the neighbouring houses, she would have spotted them as soon as she looked out of the window. She had a good view of the road from her bedroom, and the houses were generously spaced apart. So where did the person go so quickly? To the front of *her* house, out of range of her view? Or *her* garden?

Another thought puzzled her even more. The car was similar to Tony's. In fact she was practically sure it was the same make of car, a Ford Mondeo.

If it *was* Tony's car, why had he dropped someone off outside? Or was someone else driving while he got out? Had he gone to search for something he'd dropped when he collected the bin bags? The bins were out of sight of her windows, so perhaps that was the explanation.

It was all very strange, but if it was Tony, she'd probably never know the reason, because she didn't intend to get in touch with him ever again. As far as she was concerned, he was history – the kind of history never to be repeated. No way would she let any man muscle his way into her life and house so easily again.

Her stomach rumbled with lack of food, and she was still cold and shivering from hanging around the bedrooms without her slippers and dressing gown. Hot chocolate was needed.

Half way down the stairs, she froze. The slight rattle and scraping sound was unmistakable. Someone was trying to open her kitchen door from the outside.

Chapter Four

"You should have phoned Geoff," Shelley said. "He would have driven round to check the house, scare them off, and sit with you for a while."

"It was probably kids. It would be a bit drastic to wake Geoff up at that hour."

"You're not a drama queen, so if you felt the need to tell me about it, I know you think it was more than kids."

Shelley stopped talking, to serve a customer. When she turned back to Gina the customer was dithering in the shop doorway, sorting her shopping bags, so in case the customer was still within earshot she leant in towards Gina and said quietly, "Have you changed the locks?"

"Yes, the locksmith came to the house first thing. I texted him after someone tried to open the door and he replied as soon as he woke up this morning. He'd finished the job by half nine."

"Good. Do you think it was Tony? Does he still have your keys?"

"I did wonder if it was Chris at first, but with the car looking identical to Tony's… What are you laughing at?"

"I'm sorry, Gina, but Chris is the least likely of your suspects."

"I don't think that's funny enough to laugh at. I'm serious. He knows the layout of my house now, and he may appear to be shy but that doesn't mean…"

Shelley's laugh grew louder. "Shy? Chris, shy?"

"Well, maybe that's not the right word. Quiet might be better, or hesitant. Anyway, I know he's a friend of Geoff's, but…"

"Chris is a copper, Gina. He's certainly not shy. Sorry to

laugh, but maybe he was quiet because he was tired after coming off a night shift, or something. It seems as though we are talking about two different people, but I think it's safe to say you can take him off your suspect list."

"Oh!" Gina bit her lip as the heat rose from her feet through her body until her cheeks burned. "He's asked me to go to a New Year's Ball with him. I thought about cancelling."

"Has he now?" Geoff came into the shop and stood behind Shelley. "That will be the Police Ball. Every year he buys tickets but avoids actually going to it. He usually volunteers to work a shift to get out of going."

"Gina had intruders around her house, Geoff. I said if it happens again she must call you."

"Too right, love. I'll sort them buggers out for you."

As reassuring as it was to know she could ask Geoff for help, she couldn't help wishing Shelley hadn't interrupted him. She wanted to hear more about Chris's aversion to Police Balls. Did he avoid any police 'do', or was it only the ball he hated? Maybe he disliked the 'black tie' thing. After all, a lot of guys hated looking like a penguin and felt uncomfortable so dressed-up. She realised she'd missed her chance of chatting more about Chris when Shelley changed the subject.

"Gina's brought some flyers in for the shop, Geoff. I said you'd take some to the club too. Maybe you and I could go and learn some sexy moves." Shelley gave an exaggerated wink.

Geoff pretended to shudder. "No disrespect, Gina, but I'll leave those fancy dancing steps to the more flamboyant. I don't mind a bit of the old jive stuff, though. If you ever do a jive class, I'd give that a go. What d'you reckon?" He gave Shelley a playful nudge. "We could be like Sandy and Danny in *Grease*."

"There's already a dance school in the area teaching jive. I can't very well set a class up at mine too. The village is too small to accommodate both of us. Why not go along to the other one? Provided I'm not working at the same time, I'd stand in for you here, if the class is held during the shop opening hours."

"You're too soft-hearted, Gina. It's a great offer, but I'd rather be taught by you than by that dragon woman at the other dancing school. Never mind, perhaps when you're established you could give us a few pointers privately, before our holidays. There's always dancing after the comedian or singer in the evening entertainment, and if Twinkle Toes here is willing to learn," Shelley hugged Geoff's rotund middle, "it would be fun to join in properly."

Shelley and Geoff broke into a chorus of *You're The One That I Want*, making a great show of the "Oo, Oo, Oo!"

Watching them wiggle towards each other made her laugh. Thank God for people like Shelley and Geoff. They almost made her forget about what had happened in the supermarket coffee shop at lunch time.

Glad of her decision to call in at Shelley and Geoff's shop on her way home, and her mood lighter after her chat with Shelley, Gina started to look forward to the ball.

Despite it being twelve days away, the childlike pleasure from the anticipation of wearing one of her dancing dresses again bubbled up. As soon as she shut her front door, she ran upstairs, opened her wardrobe doors and surveyed her dresses.

There was everything from a short straight body-con dress to long ballroom layers of chiffon and beads. What would the other women wear? After pulling out a few dresses that would suit both formal dancing and a casual event, she settled on a knee-length taffeta and silk dress in jade green, round-necked but not low-cut, with a fitted bodice and a good swirl to the skirt without being too full. Her range of nail varnish in the bathroom cabinet didn't contain a jade colour, so she chose a pewter shade to match her shoes, and put them together ready for the ball.

Now that she knew Chris could be trusted and wasn't a stalker, it surprised her how genuinely pleased she felt that he'd asked her to go to the ball. She was looking forward to being with him, but as she made her way downstairs again, her mind switched to Lucy. She frowned.

She'd stopped for lunch in the supermarket café after giving out her flyers at various shops in the village. As she rose from her chair to move away from the table, a tall thin woman blocked her way.

"You've got a cheek delivering these around here!" The woman held Gina's flyer within inches of her face, but before she could push it away, the woman tore it up and threw it at her. The small pieces floated to the floor. "Trying to steal my students."

"I think you'll find that I will not be stealing your students. You don't teach Argentine tango. I deliberately chose something you don't teach." She was aware of the customers watching them. The café and supermarket were packed; probably people panic-buying for the New Year celebrations.

"Huh! You say that now, but I bet once you start, it won't be enough for you. There isn't room around here for two dance schools." The woman leaned in as she spoke, and cold, hard eyes stared into her own. Was she threatening her? Then she spun around and stalked off, leaving Gina on her own, the focus of the packed tables around her.

Shaking, she crouched to pick up all the torn pieces of her flyer from the floor.

It was an automatic reaction, but it gave her some time to collect herself and gather up her pride from where it had been knocked along with the other scraps. Straightening and without looking at the customers, she pulled herself up to her full five feet two inches and walked towards the exit.

Her eyes were focused on the door, except for a brief glance she wished she hadn't made, when she spied Lucy standing in the baking ingredients aisle.

This spurred her on towards the exit and into the cold fresh air. Only then did she realise she'd been holding her breath from the moment she started walking. She gasped a few times before breathing normally, waited for the faint feeling to wear off, and carried on walking.

Odd that Lucy should be in the baking aisle. She loathed baking, hated anything putting her nails in danger of being broken or messed up. Had she simply stopped there when she saw the fiasco playing out in the cafe? If so, how much had she heard? Gina wanted nothing more to do with Lucy, and certainly didn't want her gloating over the awkward confrontation. Her imagination played out Lucy telling Tony the whole sordid story, and them laughing together. Not that she could do much about it if they were, but it hardened her determination to make a success of her plans.

It took her a few seconds to realise that the jaunty tune was her mobile phone, and she dashed into the kitchen.

She didn't recognise the number on the screen and wasn't in the mood to fend off the sales pitch from a cold caller. Just before she rejected the call, she realised the caller could be a prospective dance student.

"Hello?"

"Gina, hi, it's Chris. I picked up a flyer from Geoff and Shelley's counter, with your mobile number on it. I hope you don't mind me calling."

"Ah, Chris! Sorry, I didn't recognise your number. Of course I don't mind. I suppose the sensible thing would have been to swap phone numbers the other night, when we made arrangements for the ball."

"You're not having second thoughts are you? Only—"

"No, no! I just meant it might have been wise, in case, you know—"

"Ah, yes, I see."

There was a silence. While she waited for Chris to speak, she tried to second-guess his reason for phoning, and decided to prompt him.

"So—?"

Disaster! She stopped speaking as she heard his voice, at the same time as her own. There was another long silence again as they each waited for the other to continue.

For God's sake. She imagined him holding the phone to his ear, looking at his feet, in the same way as he had hesitated when he stood at her door. Was it always going to be like this? His voice broke into her thoughts.

"...and it seemed a good idea at the time. Now I think of it, though, maybe we need to book somewhere. What do you say? Obviously if you *are* free later and if you *do* want to meet up, of course."

Oh, hell! She couldn't ask him to repeat the bit she missed. She'd have to blag it.

"If you can book, that would be preferable, I suppose." Had she said the right thing?

"So you'll come? Great, I'll phone around, see what I can arrange, and pick you up at three thirty-ish. My shift starts at seven, so I'm afraid I'll have to drop you back home about half five."

Not knowing where she was going, or indeed, what she had agreed to, she didn't know what to wear. She checked her watch. Just enough time to shower and wash her hair.

Would a smart casual outfit suit the occasion? What would he wear? A fleeting image of him in his cotton canvas jeans, that accentuated his neat bum, sparked a familiar flutter in her stomach at the anticipation of seeing him again.

It was closer to three-thirty than she thought when she finished drying her hair. She quickly chose a pair of smart navy trousers, a peach vest top, and a soft peach silk long-sleeved blouse.

Her stomach knotted as she paced the floor waiting for Chris to arrive. She hadn't been on a first date for years. Was this a date? Or was it just a friendly offer to keep her company on New Year's Eve?

"Oh, please God, don't let it be because he feels sorry for me." She spoke out loud to her reflection in the hall mirror. "I can't bear pity." She tucked a stray piece of hair behind her ear. Maybe he was lonely, too, and thought because she'd accepted his invite to the ball, she would readily accept his offer again.

For the third time in as many minutes, she checked all the doors were locked, blinds closed, and curtains drawn. The doorbell sounded as she stood in the kitchen, dithering over leaving the light on or off. She grabbed her coat.

Chapter Five

"I booked us a table at *The Natterjack* pub restaurant on the dual carriageway," Chris said as they set off in his small silver Peugeot. She couldn't help but notice how clean it was inside. Not a trace of old parking tickets, empty water bottles, plastic bags, or any of the other rubbish that used to clutter Tony's car.

"Depending on the speed of the food service, it may mean we'll have less time for the meal. I really do need to be home in time to shower and change for work."

"That's not a problem, I'm glad of the company for a couple of hours. It breaks up a long day. Is this one of the busiest nights of the year for you? Do they cancel all leave on New Year's Eve, so they have enough police to spread around?"

"You know?" Chris glanced around at her. His mouth turned up at the corners. "Someone's grassed me up! Well, it's a fair cop."

She laughed as he chuckled. He really did have the most boyishly handsome face when he let his guard down.

"I imagine we had the same informant."

"I can understand how easily I found your phone number on flyers at the shop, but how did you and Shelley, or Geoff, get onto the subject of my job?"

For a moment she wondered if Chris was annoyed that his secret, if it was a secret, had been revealed to her, but one look at his face told her he was genuinely interested in why his name had cropped up. He appeared relaxed, certainly more so than at any other time in her company. He caught her studying him and grinned, and she noticed how fresh and open his face was.

"It's a long story, and I feel really bad about one part of it.

Do you still want to know?"

"Now you have me even more curious. I think you'd better spill the beans." He turned to glance at her again. "But only if you want to tell me, of course. No pressure."

Should she tell him that she'd thought, at one point, he might be the intruder? What would he think of her? She took a deep breath. There was only one way to find out. She started to recount the goings-on outside her house on the night he had called. He listened carefully, only interrupting her once to ask who had spare keys.

They arrived in the car park of the pub before she'd finished, and he turned the ignition off and undid his seatbelt. She followed his lead with the seatbelt, and reached for the door handle.

"No, carry on. We still have a few minutes before our reservation time. Tell me the rest."

His brows had furrowed, and creases appeared around his eyes, where before he'd had laughter lines. He seemed genuinely concerned for her safety.

"Go on." He nodded towards her in encouragement.

"That's more or less all, but after the car disappeared down the road, I decided to make another hot chocolate. When I was part-way down the stairs, I heard the back door handle being turned."

"What happened then?"

"I sat on the stairs for over an hour until I was sure there was no one around, texted the locksmith, and then went to bed." She hadn't admitted that part to Shelley and Geoff, and wasn't even sure why she had just confessed to Chris. She'd been shaking so much with the fear, and unable to think straight, so when she'd eventually calmed and gathered her senses enough to think about getting the locks changed, she'd sent two garbled texts before sending a legible one.

Chris was still looking at her, waiting patiently for her to deal with the memory and carry on. She breathed deeply, missed out the altercation in the supermarket, and launched straight into telling him about her conversation with Shelley.

"You thought it was me? Wow! I must have made some

impression on you, and obviously not the right one. Are you sure you want to be out with me?"

"I feel really bad about suspecting you. I am sorry. I didn't mean to offend you, but put yourself in my place. I haven't had any trouble like this before, and on the same day as meeting you…"

"Don't worry about offending me. I understand totally, and yes, it pays to be wary of strangers, especially a dodgy-looking policeman turning up so late in the evening."

His eyes sparkled as he laughed. Thankful he hadn't taken it the wrong way, she chuckled as they left the car and headed across the car park to the entrance.

The noise met them as they entered the porch, and reached a higher level as they opened the pub door. Children ran around tables like free-range chickens, unchecked by their parents. Staff carrying trays of food and drink dodged the small darting bodies, skilfully avoiding a collision. She couldn't see an empty table, but noticed Chris mouth to her to follow him to the bar.

Whole families added to the noise, shouting to each other across long tables. Her heart sank. How was she going to get to know more about Chris, if they couldn't hear each other talk? She didn't relish the thought of shouting her way through the meal. They were led to a small table in a dark corner which, thankfully, had the advantage of being away from most of the large groups.

Chris went to the bar to order their food and drink, and returned with a tray. "I can't believe we're celebrating New Year's Eve with a pot of tea for two and hundreds of burger-eating pre-school kids!" He put the tray on the table and chuckled. "It's a good job this isn't a first date, or my chances of getting a second would be slim."

While she laughed with him, her mind worked overtime. At least that was one question answered: they weren't on a date. So did he think of them as friends, or was he doing his good deed for the day by entertaining her on one of the worst days of the year to be lonely? But why should he?

She realised he was talking to her, and apologised.

"You looked so deep in thought, I said 'Penny for them.' Are you still distressed over the intruder incident? You should lodge a report at the station, you know. If there are other incidents like yours in the area, they could be linked."

"That didn't occur to me. I just thought it was a one-off thing. I'd rather forget about it now."

"Okay." He paused for a couple of seconds. "So are you all set up for your dance class at home?"

"As much as I can be. Obviously I need students to teach, and so far four people have shown an interest. I could also do with some cheap floor-to-ceiling mirrors. They would make the room appear professional, and more like a dance studio."

"What gave you the idea for teaching Argentine tango? Not just teaching, I mean the actual dance."

Could she tell Chris the real reason, or stick with the practical one?

"Although my lounge is larger than usual, I couldn't consider anything that promenades the length of a ballroom, like a quickstep, for instance, and I don't want to be a rival to the dance school in the village. The woman who runs that doesn't teach Argentine tango, salsa or sequence dances."

She stopped talking when she noticed Chris looking thoughtful.

"Sorry, am I boring you?"

"Not at all. Carry on."

Should she tell him? She drew in a long, slow breath, and held it for a few seconds before quietly letting it out. He was smiling in encouragement.

"When I went in search of Tony at that party, you were at…"

When she hesitated, Chris leant in towards her, elbows on the table, ready to listen to whatever she wanted to say. She could smell his aftershave, and imagined his warm cheek next to hers and his breath on her neck.

"Yes?" He encouraged her to carry on with a nod of his head, his eyes fixed on hers.

She swallowed; once she started telling him, she knew she'd have to carry on. She needed to say it out loud, needed to grasp the reason behind her initial reaction that evening.

"I didn't know where Tony was, or how long he'd been out of the room. I was too busy talking to a guy in the same line of work as him. The guy was interested in offering him a job, and Tony had been looking for a change for a while."

"I saw you talking to the bloke in the expensive-looking grey suit. Was that him?"

"Yes." How long had he been watching her? She didn't recall seeing him in the thick of the party, only by the door when she was on her way out.

"I searched the downstairs rooms for Tony, and then went upstairs. I opened the bedroom door, where all the coats had been left, and saw a couple on the bed." She paused whilst she decided how to phrase the next part. "The way their legs were positioned, wrapped around each other, and the smooth movements between them…" She swallowed again. "Their bodies were perfectly synchronised and they were obviously intimate partners, and… Well, it made me think of Argentine tango."

Chris's gaze was fixed on her. Was he trying to read behind her words, using his police training, or was he genuinely absorbed in her tale?

"Stupid, wasn't it? My first thought was, if they were my students, I could train and choreograph them to win awards in that dance category."

Her eyes welled up, and he leant in closer. A waft of Patchouli teased her heightened senses.

"And then they moved apart slightly and I saw the woman was Lucy. I didn't have to wait for her partner to turn around to know it was Tony, but he did, and it was. The rest you know."

Chris shifted his arm slightly to reach out to her, and briefly brushed her hand with his, before letting it hover a few inches off the table. She willed him to take her hand and hold it. No words were needed; she just wanted to feel a connection with him. If he offered her sympathy, the dam would break and she'd embarrass herself in the middle of a full pub. She moved her hand to her lap to save him having to choose whether to touch or not. She thought quickly.

"I didn't really notice you until I was leaving. How do you know Lucy?"

There, she'd said it. Earlier, while he was ordering their meal at the bar, she'd realised she didn't know who he was with at the party. If he was married, Shelley and Geoff would surely have warned her off him, but he could have a girlfriend they didn't know about.

"I don't. My neighbour went to school with her. He was invited to Lucy's party and suggested I tag along. I believe he and Lucy were an item some years ago."

They were interrupted by the arrival of their meal and the usual list of questions about sauces and condiments from the young waiter. Chris changed the subject as they started to eat.

"I think I may be able to help you with your mirror search. Remember the day centre that closed down, on the opposite corner of the road to the station?"

She nodded. "By the park?"

"That's the one. There's been some vandalism, only minor at the moment, but we've insisted the building is made secure to stop squatters moving in. Anyway, that's all by the by, but what might be of more interest to you is the room they used as a kind of sensory area. It has floor-to-ceiling mirrors."

She raised her eyebrows. "Are they for sale?"

"During the vandalism some of the mirrors were smashed, and the shards were used in a drug-fuelled fight just before Christmas. If they haven't already been removed and destroyed, I can make enquiries about removing them for you to recycle. It's a shame to waste them, especially since you need some."

"If they don't want too much money for them, they could be perfect."

"They'll probably let you have them for free, if you can arrange to pick them up. Remind me to measure your walls when I drop you off, and I'll check. I imagine they'd be difficult to adapt if they're too big." He checked his watch. "Talking of dropping you off, I'm really sorry, but we'll need to leave in about ten minutes. I can't believe how fast the time has gone."

After they finished their meal, they returned to the car, and set off for home.

"Did you love him?" Chris asked as he turned into her road. "Tony, I mean."

The question came out of the blue after they'd travelled in companionable silence for the return journey. She thought for a couple of seconds.

"Yes, I *did*." Looking back she realised he had more faults than she thought, but when he first moved in she couldn't imagine life without him. "Why do you ask?"

"No reason. Curious." He tapped the edge of the steering wheel. "I just wondered."

The tapping continued. She watched his fingers and knew something was bothering him.

"Have you forgiven Lucy, or spoken to her?"

"No, I can't forgive Tony, so it goes without saying—"

"I could have sworn I saw her crossing the road from your house as I arrived this afternoon, but I must have been mistaken. I only met her briefly on Boxing Day. I thought I might have interrupted, or prevented you two from talking."

"Lucy? Outside my house? Except for seeing her from a distance at the supermarket in the week, I haven't seen her and I don't want to. Are you certain it was her?"

"No, I couldn't be sure." He winked, then grinned. "Certainly wouldn't swear to it in a court." His face straightened again as his voice became serious. "I just hoped you didn't change any plans you had for today because of me."

"I didn't have any plans." She regretted the sharp tone in her voice, but Chris ignored it.

"I'll measure up and be gone," he went on, as he pulled up outside her house.

She opened the front door and led him into the lounge. Using a mini tape measure from his key ring, he measured the walls and made notes on his phone.

"I need to go. Thanks for your company this afternoon. I'll see you a week on Saturday."

He slid past her on his way out of the front door, and then turned back.

"Happy New Year, Gina." He made as if to shake her hand, but quickly leant in to give her a brief and very awkward hug.

Too late, she tried returning the hug, but he moved away and set off down the path.

"Happy New Year," she called as he reached the gate.

He gave her a friendly wave, but didn't look back once he reached his car.

Her shoulders slumped. Feeling more alone than she had earlier in the day, she closed the door, walked to the hall table and leant against it.

"I shouldn't have snapped at him," she muttered to her reflection in the mirror. She thought of the shared moments. He was easy to talk to, but their conversation had been mostly about her, so had he been bored? He hadn't even said he was looking forward to seeing her again. "I expect he'll call me later to give me the brush-off, and cancel the ball event."

Chapter Six

"You've had your first class here now, haven't you? Did many turn up?"

Shelley placed her wine glass on the table and reached for a handful of nuts from the dish, before settling back into the sofa.

"I was really disappointed. Out of all the phone calls asking for details, only four turned up. Four's better than none, though, and I think it went well." Gina took a sip from her glass. "I'll know next week, won't I? I could be here on my own with egg on my face."

"I doubt that. Did that young guy from the newspaper turn up? He sounded a cert from what you told me."

"He was the first to knock. I was waiting impatiently behind the door and he arrived about fifteen minutes early. I had to count to ten before I opened it so that I didn't appear too keen." She laughed as she remembered her first sight of the broad smile on Darren's face, and his flame-red hair which flopped down over his forehead.

"Are you going to let me in on the joke?"

"Oh, Shelley, he was such a fun person and a great ice-breaker. I was glad he was the first to arrive. He stood on the door step, flung his arms in the air and announced: 'I can't wait to get started.' Then, still with his hands in the air, he jiggled his hips in a circular motion, and breezed past me into the hall! Before I closed the door I looked over to Mrs Renwick's. She was there nosing, as usual. I wish you could've seen her face. I thought she was going to have apoplexy!"

Shelley laughed, reached for more nuts and her wine, and sat back again.

"Tell me more. How did the others get on with him? What were they like?" She winked at Gina. "Was there a nice fit man for you to dance with?"

"No. There was a nice guy, although a bit quiet." She thought of the taller of the two men who arrived after Darren. He had a shaven head, and wore a tight short-sleeved T-shirt despite the freezing cold evening, with well-defined muscles under the stretch fabric. "His name is Jonathon. Darren tried to shorten it to Jon but was corrected immediately. He has a kindly face, very polite, nice smile, and he arrived with his partner Basil, an older man."

She twirled the stem of her wine glass whilst thinking about Jonathon's partner. They didn't seem suited at all. The older man – smaller than Jonathon, plump, with a receding hairline, and the rest of his unkempt hair coated with grease – remained unsmiling throughout the lesson. "I'm not sure what to make of Basil. He came over as very domineering, bossy, you know the sort, a bit of a know-it-all. Very early in the lesson, he even argued with me over one of the steps." She finished the dregs of wine left in her glass and fetched the rest of the bottle from the kitchen.

"More?"

"Please." Shelley delved in her bag and brought out more nuts and crisps, which she opened and shook into the bowls on the table between them.

"Luckily, there was one woman on her own for Darren to partner, but she's a pensioner. Forty-five years older than Darren. They did the sums, not me. On the plus side, Dorothy is a young sixty-eight-year-old. Lovely woman. Widowed. She and Darren hit it off immediately."

"Wish I'd been a fly on the wall. Somehow I can't imagine that pair dancing the Argentine tango, not seriously anyway."

"There is something I'm still worried about. I couldn't shake it out of my mind all lesson. Maybe you could ask Geoff for me, and see what he thinks. It sounds daft, but I'm not sure what to do about the front door. I don't want to be backwards and forwards as people arrive, because it will interrupt the lesson if they arrive late. If I get more students arriving, I'll need to leave it open so the students can come in, but I don't want any unsavoury intruders being able to walk in too."

"I could ask Geoff," Shelley grinned, "or you could ask Chris. He should know what to do, with being in the police. How are you getting on with him, by the way? Have you been on a date yet?"

"A date? We're just friends. We had a lunch and he found me some mirrors, the ones I showed you in the front room, but that's all. He only wants to be friends, too. What? Why are you smirking?"

"Oh, come on, Gina, it's obvious. He fancies you. And judging by your beetroot cheeks, I'd say you feel the same."

Gina shifted on the sofa, crossed and re-crossed her legs. "Whatever." When Shelley gave her an amused, knowing look, she cringed. "Can we change the subject?"

"Maybe he's waiting until the ball, when you're both in posh outfits and it'll seem more romantic. Like Cinderella. Okay, okay, I'll change the subject." Shelley winked again. It seemed to be a habit when she wanted to say more, and her eyes twinkled with mischief, too. But there was no malice in her, and Gina was glad she'd invited her around for the evening.

"Have you heard the new Bren Rourke single?" Shelley continued.

"Better than that, I've got his new album already. I'll put it on."

"You were quick off the mark. It only came out last month."

"Tony gave it to me it for Christmas." She moved towards the rack of CDs. "In fact, it was the only thing he bought me."

"Bloody hell, Gina. All those parcels you ordered for him, that you had delivered to our shop, and he just gave you a CD? Girl, you are *so* better off without him." Shelley put one hand on her hip and stretched her other arm out in front of her, pointing her finger she wagged it from side to side. "Your Chris will treat you so much better, so get a move on and net him before another girl does."

"He's not my…" Gina laughed at the raised eyebrows and comical face Shelley was making.

As she ran her fingers along a row of CDs, she reflected on the last time she'd seen Chris. He'd arrived at her door, apologetic as usual, and relieved that she was at home. Not only had he managed to procure the mirrors for her, he'd roped in a neighbour with a van to pick them up and deliver them to her house.

She opened the cabinet to place the CD in the player. It was a stereo unit that had belonged to her gran, and despite being twenty years old was still in excellent condition. The guitar started up and *One Day Like This* played softly from the speakers.

"He's certainly more thoughtful, but he's a puzzle, too. Once they'd unloaded and carried the mirrors through from the van to the room, the neighbour went off to work and left Chris here. He'd brought his drill and workbox and wasted no time putting the mirrors on the wall, there and then. After he finished, it was lunchtime, so I offered him a drink and a snack, but he declined. He said he couldn't stay and rushed off."

"Maybe he was due in work."

"No. I asked him that. His shift started seven in the evening. He muttered something about the supermarket, and before I could say more, he was out of the door and he walked home."

"Walked?"

"He'd arrived in the van with his neighbour."

"Oh yes, of course. Well, if you ask me, I think he went above and beyond the call of duty for someone who's just a friend. Wonder if I could ask him to come around to our place and put some extra shelves in the bathroom for me? I've been asking Geoff for months."

Gina marvelled at how easy it was to relax with Shelley. They must have been together drinking and chatting for almost two hours, but the time had gone so quickly that the hours had shrunk to minutes without them noticing. She couldn't help but compare it to her evenings with Lucy, who'd been her friend since they started at the high school. Lucy's conversation consisted of celebrity gossip, nail products, make-up, the latest mascara, and clothes. She had no interest in dance, wildlife, or anything else in Gina's life. Except Tony, obviously.

Shelley was a more recent friend. They'd started chatting when Shelley and Geoff took over the shop. About eighteen months ago, when Shelley received a call from the hospital saying her mum had been admitted, Gina had offered to look after the shop, so they could rush off to the hospital. Shelley had been grateful, and they had become firm friends. So why, Gina wondered, had she left it until now to invite Shelley round to her home for a quiet night in?

"Penny for them?" Shelley was watching her closely.

"I was thinking about Lucy. Why did she see Tony behind my back when she was supposed to be my friend?" She hadn't meant to voice her thoughts, but the words were out now.

"Perhaps the word 'supposed' is the clue. I always thought she was a strange friend for you, because she was obviously more concerned about herself and her appearance than about anyone else. Whereas you have a heart of gold and are always there for friends and neighbours: running errands, minding children or pets. I still remember the winter just after we moved here. You were in the shop waiting to pay and listening to old Mr Jenkins telling us his boiler was broken, so he'd no hot water or heating until the gas man could get the parts. You invited him to stay at yours for a few days until the boiler was fixed. The poor old sod thought he'd died and gone to heaven! He had three good meals a day cooked for him, a warm house, and a lovely young lady for company. He told us he felt like crying when they fixed his heating and he had to go home. Geoff and I often comment on it. There's not many around here who'd have offered their home to someone they didn't know, old gent or not."

Shelley poured what was left in the bottle between their two glasses and shook the last drops of the wine bottle into her own glass.

"I suppose Tony has moved in with Lucy?" she asked.

"I assume so. I still had his spare car key when I threw him out, and I sent it to Lucy's address. He must have received it or he'd have been in touch to ask for it back."

Shelley sucked in a deep breath before leaning forward.

"Do you want to know what I think? Well, it doesn't matter, I'm going to tell you anyway. I think you've filed Tony away in your 'in the past' folder, and you're ready to move on. The problem, as I see it, is that perhaps Chris thinks you need more time. He may be trying hard not to push you into making a rebound decision or something. If I'm right, hats off to him for being sensitive enough to give you time and space. Having said all that, you two might go on avoiding the dating thing if you don't let him know you're ready to move on."

Geoff arrived to pick Shelley up at eleven o'clock. Gina wished she could have stayed longer, but they had an early morning start at their shop. She closed the door, considered going to bed, but her head still buzzed with Shelley's advice.

She opened the door of the front room. She hadn't yet got used to calling it the dance studio. The soft glow from a street lamp a few doors away meant she didn't need to turn the light on. Moving to the middle of the floor she danced a few steps from the routine she intended to teach in the week.

As she relaxed her movements flowed and she added little touches here and there. Satisfied with the results, she turned towards the mirrors, to watch herself go through the routine again, checking for areas she could improve.

Hers wasn't the only face she saw. Reflected in the mirror, a man's face stared in through her window.

Frozen to the spot, with her heartbeat pounding loudly in her ears, she tried to scream. But the sound died in her throat, and all that escaped her lips was a rasping breath.

Chapter Seven

By the time Gina had recovered from her shock and her nerves had settled enough to look towards the window, the face had gone.

Cautiously, she ventured to the side of the curtains and peered around them. The garden and road were quiet, with no sign of anyone hanging around. She texted Shelley to ask if they'd spotted anyone wearing a hooded top, along the road, when they drove off.

Shelley replied immediately to confirm they hadn't, and added *But we weren't looking out for anyone. Why? What's happened?*

Gina sent another text with a brief explanation, ending *Not to worry. If there was someone, they've gone now.*

She hated having to close the curtains. Even her gran used to leave them open. They lived at the end of a cul-de-sac, and hardly any cars or people came as far as the end of her avenue so she enjoyed the privacy. It was lovely to have the glow from the street lamp, or the moon, entering through the window to fill the room. But now she closed the curtains in all the downstairs rooms and went up to bed.

Less than five minutes later, the sound of a car outside made her jump. She waited, wondering whether to get up to look out of the window. "Not again," she muttered. Her whole body tensed, wondering if it was the silver saloon car again.

As she sat on the edge of the bed, her mobile phone pinged.

Hey, Gina, she read, *it's Geoff. I'm outside. Had a good look around. There's no one here, either in your road or garden. Sleep well. Any worries, PHONE US!*

She rushed to the window and looked out.

Geoff stood by the door of his car, looking up. When he saw her at the window, he made a 'thumbs-up' sign and waved. She waved back and mouthed, "Thank you," hoping he would see. He nodded, got in the car and drove off. She texted her thanks to him and settled down.

After a restless night, she checked around the outside of her house again. Nothing seemed amiss, but she was thankful she'd had the house locks changed. At least that was one thing less to worry about.

As she was washing her breakfast crockery, a knock at the front door startled her.

The first thing she saw as she opened the door was a police car parked outside. To her surprise, Chris stood at the side of the bay window in his uniform.

Her heart gave a little jump, and then fluttered. The uniform suited him. No, not *suited*, that was the wrong word. Her gran would say, it *became* him. She'd never had a 'thing' for a man in uniform, but now she could understand that some women did!

"Hello, I wasn't expecting to see you. Is everything ok?" Her first thought was he'd come to say they couldn't go to the ball, but surely he would wait until he was off duty?

"I believe you had another intruder last night."

This was a Chris she hadn't seen before. There was none of the hesitancy, apologies for inconveniencing her, or fidgeting. This Chris was confident, looked her in the eye, and (with a surprisingly authoritative tone) came straight to the point. All that, whilst still appearing heart-crushingly handsome in his uniform.

Before she could switch her mind to what he was saying, and try to form a simple sentence in response, he went on, "I called in at the shop on the way to work, and Geoff told me about your text. He was worried, and rightly so. You should have reported it."

"What if it was my imagination playing tricks? I can't call the police every time I think I see someone hanging around."

"But you can text your friend? If you were sure enough to

get in touch with Shelley, you should have made a quick call to the station. If they had a car in the area, they would have asked them to patrol down here."

She shook her head. "It was a face. A man with a stubble-type beard, wearing a hoody. He didn't try the doors, or do any damage outside."

Chris's eyes widened. "You went outside?"

"No, not last night. I checked this morning."

His shoulders relaxed slightly, and his soft barely audible sigh showed how worried he was.

"Gina, please report it. This is the second incident. If it's connected to your first one, it needs investigating. Even if it is a separate incident, there might be someone in Freshby having a similar problem with the same guy. We could link them together. I can mention it at the station, but I can't investigate it because of our – erm – our friendship." His radio crackled, and he automatically touched it, ready to press the button. "Be careful, Gina. Report it." He nodded to her as if willing her to nod in agreement. As his radio crackled again, he turned to walk towards the car.

"I'll call in later, on my way to the shops," she said.

He held his hand up. Was that a thumbs-up? She couldn't be positive. What was positive though, was the deflated sensation in her chest. She could still breathe, but someone was trampling all over her heart and lungs, making it painful to catch her breath, and difficult to stay happy, even at the sight of him in uniform.

If only he'd said something nice to her before he walked off. He'd been so official and detached. No, that wasn't a fair description. He obviously cared, or he wouldn't have turned up at her door urging her to involve the police. Maybe she was expecting too much of him? After her chat with Shelley, was she hoping he'd open up to show his real feelings? But he'd only referred to their 'friendship'.

She could only hope that the situation between them would become clearer at the weekend, during the charity ball.

At precisely eight o'clock the doorbell rang.

Gina had been dressed and waiting for an hour. She opened the door, and the sight of Chris in his dinner suit and bow tie took her breath away.

Not knowing what to say to distract from her obvious surprise and pleasure, she managed a self-conscious grin. "Will I do?"

He struggled to speak, but the admiration in his eyes told her what she needed to know, until he found his voice.

"Stunning." His voice, soft and sincere, boosted her confidence and calmed her nerves. "I didn't mean to make you blush, but you do. Look stunning I mean. Beautiful."

Her cheeks burned and she hoped her complexion spray fared better during the evening than it had on the doorstep. When had Tony last paid her a compliment like that?

"Ready?" He offered her his arm.

He was quiet in the taxi. Partly to break the silence, she said, "You certainly suit the dinner jacket ensemble. Very *James Bond*."

"A bit cheesy, then?"

She opened her mouth to protest but stopped when she saw him smile, and nudged his side. "Stop fishing for more compliments. You look great."

He sat back in his seat, and she sensed him relaxing. If she asked him now, he might give her a truthful answer and then she would know what to avoid during the evening.

"Why don't you like the New Year Ball? And why buy tickets if you didn't intend to go?"

For a moment he tensed. She thought he wasn't going to answer and rehearsed a quick apology in her head.

"Pressure," he said.

She gave him a quizzical look, willing him to expand.

"That's it really. I buckled under pressure to buy them. I didn't want to be the bad guy that refused. The money raised goes to charity, so even if I didn't attend, the money isn't wasted."

"Why not go if you have the tickets?"

"Pressure," he said again, but this time he didn't tense. Instead there was a mischievous glint in his eyes. "The pressure of having to find someone as stunning as you to take along."

"Whoa! Too cheesy! Definitely too *James Bond*."

As he laughed with her, a warm tingle rippled through her.

Certain now that her decision to accept his invitation had been right, she looked out of the window, waiting for the lights of Dunesands Hall to come into view.

As they drove down the long sweeping drive to the hotel building, he reached for her hand and squeezed it. She left it nestled in his until he released it as the taxi pulled up outside the entrance and a concierge came forward to open the car door for her.

Chris was soon at her side, offering her his arm again, not reaching for her hand. Maybe he thought it too intimate for a first date. Was it a first date? Or was it simply a convenient arrangement?

A sense of deflation took her by surprise. After all, she was the one who had wanted it to be casual, with a get-out-early clause. Did he feel the same way? She snuck a quick glance in his direction, only to look away when she realised he was watching her.

He patted her hand which rested on his arm.

"Ready to face the rabble?"

She had been so engrossed in working through her feelings that she hadn't noticed the open doors leading to the ballroom.

The Dunesands Hall Hotel & Health Club was way out of her budget. It was the sort of place where the wives of the rich or famous chose to be seen at each week. Looking at the crystal light fixtures and huge pendant lights, Gina couldn't help but think *cheap bling,* but no doubt they were the real thing and cost a fortune. Everything was impressive, albeit over the top, positively ostentatious, and definitely over-priced. The only fake thing about the hotel was probably the clientele.

She drew in a deep breath as she braced herself for an evening of false smiles and insincerity. "Ready." Down by her side, she crossed the fingers of her free hand.

"Chris! What a surprise! You actually made it here! Didn't

they have a shift for you to work this year?"

With her arm still linked in his, she felt a slight movement as Chris stiffened and pressed her arm into his body. She moved her free hand to place it on top of his, willing him to relax.

"Hi. I'm Gina. And you are…?"

A startled look crossed the big guy's face as she addressed him, but her interruption succeeded in diverting the prospect of more snide remarks aimed at Chris, as he turned his attention to her instead.

"Terry, good friend of Chris's." Another tense movement from Chris. "He kept you quiet."

Terry's smirk presumably meant *So he managed to find someone to bring at last.*

Her reply was smooth and quick. "That was my fault. I insisted he did." She turned to Chris. "Shall we find a table? How about that one over there, unless you have another preference?" She pointed to the furthest empty table from Terry and his group.

"That'll be fine." Chris followed her lead. "If you want to go and claim the table, I'll join the queue at the bar."

"Will do," she said with a smile, and added, "I'll have my usual, darling." She nodded at Terry and turned to make her way towards the empty table before Chris could ask her what her usual was. He would have to use his imagination.

"Did I make it so obvious that I didn't want to talk to Terry?" he whispered a few minutes later, as he placed a white wine in front of her, and raised his eyebrows. "Your usual, darling?"

She wasn't sure whether he was questioning the choice of drink or her use of the word 'darling', but took a sip and held up her glass to clink his.

She smiled. "Perfect. Cheers! Here's to an interesting evening."

"How did you guess?"

"Elementary, my dear Watson." She gave him an exaggerated wink. "Your body language gave me a clue. I hope you're better at questioning than being questioned."

He found his feet interesting once again. This was becoming a habit. Did she make him nervous, or did he have something to hide?

"Joking, not accusing. Chris, what's the deal here? Terry, for instance? Good friend or not a friend?"

"Not a friend."

"I got that right then. Asking me to the ball, regret or no regrets?"

He reached for her hand and squeezed it gently. "Definitely no regrets."

Across the room she caught sight of Terry's table. He pointed towards her and Chris, and said something that made the group around him laugh. Another man at the table rose from his chair. Oh God, he was walking in their direction.

The band was playing, and she turned quickly to Chris. "Do you waltz, Chris?"

"A little."

"Then let's do a little waltz." She smiled at him, and held out her hand.

She thought he might object. Tony didn't dance at all unless he was tanked up with drink, and then it was more a case of leaning on her and shuffling. He would never have forgiven her for leading him on to a half-empty dance floor.

Chris made no such protests, but taking her hand, willingly led her to the middle of the floor. She couldn't help but be impressed with his straight back, firm hold and tilted chin. He held her so close she could feel the contours of his body. Her nerve endings were sent into a pleasurable overdrive, and she had to use all her self-control to focus on the music. A ripple of delight ran through her as soon as he stepped forward with his left foot, because it was immediately apparent he knew more than the 'little' bit of waltz he admitted to.

In response to his posture, she leant back into his supporting hand and turned her head to the left.

She let him guide her around the floor. It wasn't a faultless performance, but he didn't follow his mistakes with profuse apologies as she would have expected. He corrected his step and carried on.

When the music stopped she waited for him to return to his beer, but he stayed on the floor, still holding her close. His warm breath and the aroma of lemons and patchouli aftershave caressed her face, and without realising it, she breathed them in wishing for the next dance to be another slow, close one, not a cha cha.

"That was just the warm-up. I think I've got it now. Another dance? I saw how you rescued me and, at this rate, we'll need to stay on the floor all evening."

Stay like this in his arms all evening? *Yes, please…*

She toned down her eagerness in her reply. "I'm happy to dance all evening if you are."

"I warn you, I only know a few dances, and your shoes look too delicate for my size tens to stand on."

She laughed. "Then hopefully I can move them out of the way in time."

The music started up with another waltz. This one was much smoother, as they adapted to each other's length of step. His hold was firm and confident.

If she were a judge, she would certainly give him an eight. Her next thought caused her to stifle a chuckle, noting that as boyfriend material, he would be right up there with top marks. She relaxed into his hold, enjoying the warmth and feel of his hand on her back. She wanted to close her fingers around his and hold her head up for him to lean in and kiss her lips. Her eyes closed briefly until she remembered where they were and how they were meant to be 'just friends.'

As the music finished, Chris turned to speak to a man who tapped him on the shoulder and asked how he was.

Gina was aware of being pushed as someone passed her. There weren't many couples on the floor, so it surprised her that the person chose to pass her so closely. She understood the reason, however, when she realised who it was.

"Don't think you are impressing everyone with your teaching abilities. What I saw was amateurish at its best, from both of you." The words were hissed at her by the owner of the Freshby Dance School. Despite being incensed, Gina was unable to make a retort without shouting it at the retreating back.

How dare she? The pleasure she'd been enjoying from dancing with Chris ebbed away, and her response to his request to join the next dance was less than enthusiastic. She would rather sit it out than make a fool of herself doing a foxtrot on the dance floor. Visions of Chris fumbling his way through the steps in an effort to follow her lead crowded her head. She was instantly sorry for her less than charitable thoughts when Chris, obviously reading her refusal as rescuing her toes from being stepped on, announced that he knew the foxtrot better than any other dance.

"My mother taught me how to foxtrot in my early teens. It was a dance my father refused to learn. That, and the jive, were the dances I did with her when they went to competitions with their dance school." He grinned and her heart jumped. "Your toes will be safe if you follow my lead. Of course, if you don't keep up, I can't guarantee you won't leave them in my path."

She laughed. Sod Mrs Freshby Dance School! She wasn't going to let her ruin the evening. So what if they looked like amateurs? She was with Chris, and dancing in a room where she wasn't teaching.

He led her to the most prominent place on the dance floor and they held their pose waiting for the music to start. She learnt back and turned her head to the left. In her direct line of vision, glaring at her with obvious venom, was the rival dance teacher. Rival seemed a harsh word, but she justified it by reminding herself that it hadn't been her choice. She added a little prayer that she and Chris wouldn't mess it up too much.

The music started, Chris put his left foot forward, and they moved along the floor. Slow, slow, quick, quick... He led her competently through step after step. She felt every rise and fall, he steered her firmly through turns, they promenaded together in time, and they were perfectly synchronised. He amazed her with his performance. He was certainly the most excellent accomplished dancer she had partnered on the ballroom floor. Her only hope was that she had done him the justice he so clearly deserved.

She needn't have worried.

The next foxtrot tune blended seamlessly with the first and they carried on without a break. She became increasingly aware of the other couples leaving the floor and forming a circle around them. Even Freshby's very own poisonous, hissing snake had left the dance floor. When the music stopped they were on their own.

A roar of appreciation and loud applause echoed around the ballroom, with some voices cheering and shouting "Encore!"

Chris's eyes twinkled with pleasure. He beamed from ear to ear and hugged her close.

She leant her head towards him and whispered, "Wow! Just wow! I haven't enjoyed dancing like that for years."

"Neither have I." His deep blue eyes gazed into hers with admiration, and he kissed the top of her head. "You were amazing. You followed my every step."

"You were a good lead. I could tell every move you were going to take next."

If only she could read his intentions as well as his dance moves...

As he lead her back to their table, she moved in a little closer, hoping for another show of affection, but at the same moment, the man he'd spoken to on the dance floor slapped him on the back and announced, "You two were made for each other. I'd pay good money to see more of that. A neatly executed Operation Foxtrot on the dance floor. Talking of which, I think you're on again."

"Come on, Gina. They're playing our song again."

She willingly let herself be guided back on to the dance floor for another foxtrot. *Our song.* They already had their very own song?

Michael Jackson sang *The Way You Make Me Feel* as they glided their way around the empty floor. Only when the music slowed to a social foxtrot did other couples rejoin them on the dance floor, and Chris led her into the circle for the sequence dance.

She was delighted with all the compliments they received from the other dancers, but her eyes were firmly fixed on

Chris. He was more animated than she'd ever seen him.

When the dance ended, he left her sitting at their table while he went to the bar for a few more drinks. She happily tapped the beat with her fingers on the table, as she watched the now full dance floor. They had decided to sit out the rest of the sequence dancing, and she was looking forward to chatting to him. Maybe he would tell her more about his mum and dad and his dancing competitions.

She smoothed her dress out from the ribs down and ruffled the skirt to let it drape neatly over her legs, but took a quick breath when the dreaded dance school woman undulated across the room towards her. The dress she wore, hologram snake foil, spandex fabric, hugging her curves, with tissue metallic lame splaying out from just above her knees, hardly moved as she made her way purposefully towards the table.

Gina's heart sank. What else was the awful woman going to say?

Chapter Eight

"I suppose you think you've proved yourself to be a professional?"

The woman waited for a reply, but Gina sat tight-lipped. Determined not to be drawn into a catfight and ruin her wonderful evening with Chris, she forced a smile in case they were being watched.

The woman went on, "You may have won tonight, but don't think you can start up a foxtrot class and steal my students."

Gina could see the woman's partner approaching, and prayed he'd whisk her away before the woman spoilt her evening.

"I wouldn't dream of it," she replied through her false smile. "It was never my intention, not in Freshby anyway."

"There you are, Paula! Are you ready to cha cha?" The woman's partner gave Gina a genuine smile. "Wonderful foxtrot, my dear. You were a pleasure to watch, wasn't she, Paula? It was perfect, couldn't fault it, even though we tried."

"I bet you tried," Gina muttered as they moved away to join in the Latin dancing. So her name was Paula. *Paula the Viper*. It felt gratifying to give her adversary a nickname. It suited her, as the forehead tiara she wore had a V shape like the markings on the snake's head. She chuckled to herself, as the thought crossed her mind, that Paula's tongue was worse than the snake's venom.

"Happy?" Chris asked as he put the drinks on the table.

"Very." Shelley's advice echoed in her mind, and she added, "I don't think I've enjoyed an evening so much for a long time."

Chris pushed his chair nearer to her and sat down. If she moved her leg forward just a few inches, their knees would be touching. She shifted slightly in her seat, but couldn't bring herself to close the distance between them. While she hesitated in an agony of indecision, Chris moved his knee against hers, and her stomach fluttered. This was what she wanted. Being close to him, sharing the evening with him, catching the scent from his aftershave, everything combined to make her so happy she wanted to twirl around like a child in a party dress.

When they weren't on the dance floor, they talked about the other dancers, and Chris told her snippets of information about his colleagues and his work. It was difficult to talk above the noise and they moved their heads closer together so they could hear each other. Occasionally they touched hands, often the lightest of touches, but each time an electric current shivered through her body. She made a point of smiling and holding his gaze each time he looked directly at her, hoping to encourage him to lean in closer and kiss her. He didn't, but he was visibly relaxed in her company. She lost track of time and was unaware of the people around them, so that when the lights eventually went up she felt as though someone had let the air out of their bubble, forcing them to float slowly back to earth.

They both let out a sigh of regret at the same time. Laughing together, he put his arm around her shoulder and drew her towards him until their foreheads and the tips of their noses touched. He said, in a voice so low it was barely audible, "That's a shame, I didn't want the evening to end."

"Neither did I." She moved her forehead away from his and tilted her chin in the hope that he might kiss her. He didn't, but instead he removed his arm from her shoulder, moved to stand behind her and waited for her to rise out of the chair, pulling it back to make it easier for her to leave the table.

She swallowed her disappointment. Not trusting herself to speak without a wobble in her voice, she thanked him, and with her head down to avoid direct eye contact, she took a little longer than necessary to rearrange the folds of her dress and pick up her bag, until she'd composed herself again. He offered her his arm, and they walked through to the foyer in silence.

In the taxi, with his arm around her, she snuggled into his

shoulder. They journeyed home in a comfortable silence but, as they approached her avenue, she wondered if she should ask him in, or wait for him to suggest it, or simply say goodnight.

Her questions were answered when they arrived outside her house and Chris got out, holding the door open for her, but telling the taxi driver to wait while he walked her to the door.

"I've had a lovely evening," she said as she stood on the step and put her key in the door.

"I'm glad I bought the tickets. You made it all worthwhile." He looked into her eyes for a moment. Her heart melted at the tender expression in them, and a surge of heat radiated through her chest. Just at the point where she thought she couldn't bear to wait for him to make a move any longer, he cupped her face in his hands, and leant forward to kiss the top of her head. Then bending his knees to move down to her level, he softly kissed her forehead, her closed eyes, her nose, and finally placed his warm lips on hers. Wrapping his strong arms around her, he pulled her against his chest as she lost herself in his kiss.

When they paused, his fingers played with her hair, gently twisting a tendril.

"I'm working for the next few days. I'll give you a call as soon as I have some time off." He looked at her hair, caught between his fingers, and ran his hand around the back of her head to tilt it up to meet his lips in a parting kiss. "Take care, Gina. See you soon."

He waited for her to unlock the door and step inside, before walking back to the taxi.

Gina had so much to think about the next morning that she went for a walk to clear her head. It was cold but fresh, and the clear blue sky made a refreshing change from the dreary rain they'd been having since November.

She chose the road that led down to the sand dunes. The wind by the sea would be cutting, but she wore a thick jumper over several layers of tee-shirts, and her ski jacket over that. She had no intention of catching a chill so early in the new year.

Her route took her past the dance school in the village. The lights were on, and, not wanting to bump into Paula, she put her head down and quickened her step. It seemed a little odd that Paula should be in her studio so early on a Sunday morning, especially after being out late the night before, but perhaps she was teaching an extra lesson, or preparing the room for her classes. Of course, it might not be Paula. It could be another teacher or student.

Annoyed at herself for taking such an interest in a woman who very clearly didn't think much of her, Gina brought her thoughts back to Chris, and *that* kiss.

Her stomach fluttered again as she relived the moment his lips met hers.

All evening, she'd hoped for such a tender ending to their date. From the minute he held her close in the waltz, his arms felt so right around her. Not just because he had the correct posture and hold, but because she felt as though being in those arms was where she belonged.

Her step was light with a little spring in it, so it took her no time at all to reach the track which led through to the sand dunes. It was her favourite route, one she used to walk with her gran.

Gran would have loved Chris. He was what Gran would have described as the 'nice young man' she was always urging her to find. Sadly, now she'd found one, Gran wasn't around to get to know him.

Chris had smiled at her a lot during the ball, especially when he looked down at her with his warm and caring blue eyes, which made her heart melt with longing. How she longed to lose herself in those eyes. He'd made her feel as if she was the only woman in the room.

"Oi! Watch it, *girl*!"

She was brought back to earth with a start, when she almost fell over an outstretched dirty sleeping bag in the path. A quick glance at the offending object showed her there was somebody sleeping in it. She looked around, and saw four unkempt men, hanging around the end of the path that led back into the woods or down to the beach. They all glared at her from under hooded parkas or pull-on beanie hats. Hanging in the air was a sickly-sweet pungent odour, a tell-tale sign of some sort of weed or drug cigarette.

She mumbled apologies and continued to walk straight ahead.

The crack of twigs, from behind her, was accompanied by the heavy breathing of someone making a laboured effort to catch up with her. She quickened her step. If he was unfit he might stop and turn back. On the other hand, if he was drugged up, he could be aggressive, and she needed to put more distance between them. The track was growing less firm underfoot, the soft sand making it difficult to walk, and the trees were now behind her. All she had in front of her was an expanse of sandhills. Her trainers were sinking into the soft loose fine sand and her progress was slowing. Lightheadedness washed over her as her legs and knees weakened with the effort of trying to get away.

He had the advantage of longer legs, and it took him no time at all to close the gap she'd gained.

A hand on her shoulder pulled at her roughly so that she fell backwards, landing on her bottom on a raised hillock of sand. Her lungs expelled all her remaining air with the shock, and she gasped for breath.

He leant over her, his eyes bloodshot with huge black pupils. As well as the obvious weed cigarette smell, he reeked of bad hygiene.

"Got some cash?"

"No, I'm only out for a walk." Glancing around, she saw how alone she was on the dunes. That wasn't something she'd had to worry about before. Normally it was a pleasant and hassle-free route for a few hours' walk, but now her racing heartbeat was deafening.

"You're lying. Who around 'ere goes out without cash? Yer all posh nobs 'ere." He leant nearer and she could feel the spray from his lips as he spoke. "I'm sure you'd like to make a... Shall we call it a 'voluntary donation'? Jus' so you can carry on with your little walk."

A black and white flash of fur, teeth and claws sailed past

her head and knocked her assailant backwards. He somehow stayed on his feet, but spun around, and covered the return distance to his mates chased by the dog. A sharp whistle pierced the air, and the dog, a Border Collie, stopped and dropped down, ready to run again.

Gina picked herself up, brushed all the sand off her clothes and rubbed her hands together to clean them.

She was still shaking when a tall grey-haired man appeared at her side. He was wearing a smart wool coat with a striped felted wool scarf tucked in at the neck. She warmed to him immediately. He shook her hand.

"Are you okay?" he asked.

"I am now, thanks to you and your lovely dog. Thank you so much for rescuing me."

"No worries, you're welcome. I've not seen that lot around here before. They usually stay down by the Old Powerhouse or the lighthouse. They can be very intimidating, especially to a girl out on her own." He whistled to his dog, who came bounding over, tongue lolling and tail wagging. The man reached into his pocket and produced a treat.

"Can I reward him?" she asked, and took the treat that was handed over. She pointed to the space in front at her feet, and issued her command. "Sit."

The Border Collie sat, eyes fixed on her. "Good boy." She held the treat out on the palm of her hand, and the dog very gently took it from her.

"I'm impressed. You know how to handle a Border Collie. My name's Richard, by the way."

"Gina." They shook hands. "My Gran and Grandad had one when I was much younger." She stroked the dog's head that was pressing against her thigh.

"A girl of many talents. Dancer and dog-tamer!"

She gave him a guarded look. How did he know she danced? And was it just a coincidence he appeared when he did?

"You were at the ball last night. Chris's partner?"

"Sorry, I didn't notice you there." She was relieved at the simple explanation. For goodness sake, she was becoming far too jumpy and suspicious.

"We left early, but not before I watched you dance. Nice footwork." Richard chuckled. "Our Chris is a bit of a dark horse, isn't he? No doubt he'll be ribbed for months for his twinkle toes."

"Oh dear, will he? But he *is* a very good dancer, isn't he?"

"No doubt about that. He put my efforts with the missus to shame, even though we dabbled in a few lessons to impress at the ball. I can't blame him for showing off a little."

"I don't think he intended to show off." She was miffed that he thought Chris came across as posing, rather than just enjoying himself. Then she regretted that her tone may have seemed rude. Thankfully he didn't seem to notice.

"Well, let's say he was probably trying to impress you. And I'd brush up on my dancing skills for someone like you, too." He briefly touched her shoulder. "Sorry, I didn't mean to make you blush. It really was good to see Chris so animated. I used to think he was far too serious for a young man. Often looked like he had all the troubles of the county weighing him down. But he's kept you quiet. Didn't know he was courting, but you seem suited for each other. Even a cynical old cop like me can see that."

Thinking it safer to keep off the subject of their relationship, she opted for something neutral to say. "I really enjoyed the evening. It's a long time since I've worn my ball gown."

"I'm glad your evening wasn't spoilt by Paula." He dropped his voice slightly, as if worried they may be overheard. "I heard what she said to you about poaching her students."

Gina opened her mouth to protest, to tell him she hadn't intended to poach anyone, and didn't wish to pick a fight with Paula, but he carried on before she could speak.

"I know what she can be like, but she hasn't always been so fierce." He stopped and rubbed his chin. "Her studio was broken into last night, and in fact when I saw her there this morning she was upset and vulnerable. I felt sorry for her, and it's not often I feel that way, but I think it's important for you to know why Paula is now the prickly person she has become."

Gina was about to object, and tell him he didn't need to explain, but he stopped her and carried on talking.

"I'm not telling you anything that isn't already known in the village. She met her husband at a dance competition. They set up a dance school in Eastbourne, and it very quickly filled and made them a lot of money. When she became pregnant, he took on another dancer to do freelance teaching, an attractive Australian girl. You can see where this is going?"

She nodded.

"He set up his own school with his new partner on the other side of the town, taking all their students with him. Paula was left with a building to pay for, no students to teach, and no rent money for somewhere to live. She threw everything she had into building up her dance school again, enough to pay the bills. Each time she managed to attract a few students, he poached them. The stress made her so ill, she lost the baby."

"Oh no! How awful!" Gina spoke with a catch in her throat. "How could he do that to her? It's despicable!"

"When she recovered her health, she had massive debts. She sold what she could, begged loans from relatives, and moved here. The thing is – she's my niece. On the one hand, I feel protective towards her; on the other, it saddens me to see how isolated she's become. Very few friends; well, genuine ones anyway. She's become a very hard person, very business-minded, and difficult to get close to. She will see you as a threat. She started her school up here, in the same way you are trying to do. In my brother's house.

"I didn't know any of that. I'll admit she certainly had me worried, but I'm not setting up in competition to her. I don't intend to teach any of the dances she offers."

"Gina, I can see you're are a lovely kind person, but if you are setting up a business, don't take any heed of her. You can't pussyfoot around; business is a cut-throat world. To succeed, you need to take risks and show determination. Paula will survive being one of two schools in the area. It is a real shame, though, that you two can't join forces and pool your talents."

"Thanks for the advice. I do appreciate it, but for now, I'll stick to teaching just the one class. Even if I wanted to offer more, my space is limited."

"Then I wish you good luck." Richard glanced to the spot behind her where the men and sleeping bag had been grouped. "They've moved on. You'll be okay to continue on your walk. Nice talking to you, Gina. Tell Chris I was asking after him."

With a final whistle to his dog to follow, he turned and walked back in the direction he'd appeared from.

Chapter Nine

Gina nursed a mug of coffee in her hand. It was eight o'clock in the morning and she'd hardly slept after returning home from work the previous evening and discovering she'd been a victim of intruders.

The police officer, who introduced himself as Mike Holmes, sat opposite her and read from his notes.

"Your neighbour, Mrs Renwick, has informed us that she saw it all happen minutes after you turned the corner of the road. She presumed you were on your way to work, because you leave the house at the same time on week-nights."

Gina nodded to acknowledge Mrs Renwick was correct. Tony used to call her 'that bloody old bag of a nosey parker,' but Gina had always insisted her neighbour was lonely.

"She's right. I always catch the six-o'clock train to Southport to get the train to Wigan where I teach my freelance classes. My first dance class is at seven-thirty, and the train journey gives me an hour to prepare the lesson, providing I can find a seat. Always difficult on peak-hour trains." She pulled a face. Standing on the trains all the way to Wigan made her legs ache, and she couldn't write notes standing up. "The stupid thing is that, as the train pulled away from the platform, I remembered the assessments file I'd left on the kitchen table. I did fleetingly think about getting off the train at the next stop. I'd have one minute to cross the station and return on the train, which would give me ten minutes to pick up the file and catch the next train to Wigan. You don't really want to know all that, do you?"

The heat flooded her cheeks. She had a habit of talking too much when she was nervous, and sitting opposite the policeman unnerved her. She wished it was Chris sitting in this man's place, holding her in a warm hug and telling her he could make everything right again. But how could he? For the umpteenth time since last night, she wished she hadn't decided against getting off the train. Sitting here going through the events of the evening, and hearing how close to catching the culprits she would have been, she realised how wonderful hindsight could be.

Mike carried on reading from his notes.

"Mrs Renwick told me, and I quote..." The officer's expression was impassive and she had no idea what he was thinking. "*I thought it unusual behaviour, because the man didn't knock at the front door, like all Miss Pendleton's other men.*"

Gina spluttered. Other men? Mrs Renwick made it sound as though she had men wearing out the path to her door.

Mike continued, "She said he went down the path that leads to the back of the house. There was a minute or so when she lost sight of him because she had to rush from the front window to the back bedroom window, so she didn't know what he did in between that time. She saw him go back to his car and drive off." He checked his notes again, "He was wearing blue jeans, black jacket and a pull-on hat, and he was driving a silver car." He turned the page, read some of it silently, and then read aloud once more.

"Your neighbour had to admit, I quote, *I have never seen any of Miss Pendleton's gentleman friends enter the house by the back door, so I presumed that wasn't his intention.*"

"Gentleman friends? I don't have gentleman friends. I had a partner for three years until we split up on Boxing Day. She makes me sound like some sort of trollop!"

Mike smiled and his shoulders relaxed.

"It's okay, Miss Pendleton, I don't think she meant it like that. She told us that as far as she could see, the men visiting you lately had – erm – feminine tendencies and probably weren't interested in you as a woman. She has apparently noticed through your front lounge window that you dance quite a lot with a few of your women visitors, and," he paused again and gave a little cough, "she wondered if you were one of *those* type of women she'd heard about in the papers."

He had the grace to look embarrassed, and she didn't know whether to be relieved or not that her neighbour wasn't tarnishing her reputation by insinuating that she was sleeping with her male visitors. It seemed a bit of a double-edged sword, especially when she realised she hadn't made it clear that her ex-partner was male.

"I'm a dance teacher," she offered by way of explanation.

Mike's expression didn't give anything away, and she saw no reason to give any further defence of her situation. It was none of his business, anyway. She decided to ask some questions of her own.

"You say my neighbour saw the car. Did she get the registration?"

"No, and she didn't know the make of the car either. She did, however, tell us that she had never seen a car like that one outside your house before."

"Did she remember the shape of the car? It seems to me that someone knows my comings and goings, otherwise how did they know I would be out the first time, and when to come back?"

She shuddered as she recalled the incident before New Year.

"They probably just took a chance. If they came back at night when there were no lights on in the house, they could presume it was safe to wander around unseen. If they were quiet, then barring guard dogs and security lights, they could go about the job unnoticed."

She wasn't convinced.

"But, if they didn't knock at the front door, how would they have known it was okay for them to wander around the back of the house the first time? Even if they saw me go out, how would they know that I lived on my own? Why did they think there would be no-one else in the house to catch them out?"

Apparently unsure of how to answer, Mike wrote a few notes in his book.

"I've made a note of your question but I doubt it's relevant. I'm sure they just found an opportune moment, but it may have some bearing on the case. In answer to your question about the car, we already have that in hand. Mrs Renwick will be shown pictures of cars to pick one similar to the one she saw."

He put his notes away and smiled. "Between you and me, usually unless they know a fair bit about cars, people who only glance at a car aren't very good at identifying them from photos. Your neighbour, however, obviously spends a great deal of time watching from her window, and invests a bit of energy into keeping an eye on movements in the road. She may surprise us, as she has been very observant so far."

Gina looked up to the heavens and shook her head.

"I'm not sure if that is a good thing or not."

"We'll be in touch. If your neighbour does manage to identify a make of car, we will need to know if it belongs to any of your friends or clients." He looked down as he said the word *clients,* as if he'd intentionally used it as a double meaning. She didn't care.

As the officer left her house, she saw Chris opening the gate. The officer acknowledged him and the two of them then lowered their voices in an exchange she couldn't hear, but once or twice she caught Chris glancing in her direction.

He continued up the path, a worried frown on his face.

She leant out of the doorway to look at her neighbour's house. As expected, Mrs Renwick was standing in her bay window. Gina waved, and the elderly woman stepped back from view. It was perhaps a good thing that her neighbour was an unofficial, self-appointed home-watch. But on the other hand, she wished Mrs Renwick would allow her some privacy.

"Why didn't you phone me? This is the third incident in a month, isn't it?" Chris's concern came through in his voice as he followed her into the house.

"You were on duty last night, and I wasn't aware until this morning that Mrs Renwick had reported it and dealt with the police while I was at work yesterday evening."

She motioned to him to sit on the sofa in the dining room, whilst she poured them both a coffee from the stove-top percolator. She didn't want to be able to see out of the kitchen window so sat on the other sofa, with her back to the kitchen.

The thought of the mess she would have to clear up was enough, without it being in full view.

"The first I knew something was wrong was when I turned the corner. I'd been held up after class so I had to catch a later train home. The road was a mess of plants and soil, broken pots and ornaments. *My* garden ornaments." She stopped. Her chest felt tight and a lump rose in her throat as she thought of her gran's pride in her garden.

"They were my gran's garden pots and ornaments. She'd collected them over the years when Grandad was alive. Many were bought as gifts to each other for birthday, anniversary and other occasions. The small statue of a kissing boy and girl was Grandad's gift to Gran, when she gave birth to my mum."

She put her hand over her mouth to stop the bile rising. Her gran's memories were embedded in those ornaments, and the mindless destruction of her garden by faceless vandals sickened her.

Chris jumped up and moved over to her, and put his arm around her shoulders.

"Mrs Renwick spotted them, but it was a while before she realised what they were doing. She rang the police, but they'd gone before anyone arrived. They've been in the shed, smashed Grandad's greenhouse, and made a huge mess of the garden."

"They? Any idea who they were? Men or boys?"

"Mrs Renwick only saw one man. But when you look at the mess, you'll see why I say 'they'. There must have been more than one to cause such devastation in a short space of time."

A large sob escaped as she spoke, and a tear ran down her cheek. She tried to brush it away, but it was instantly replaced by more.

"I spent last night rescuing the broken stoneware and plants with roots. I've been out this morning, taking photos, surveying the damage in the garden, and finding all the other broken pieces of memories. I had the stupid idea of trying to glue or cement them back together." She shook her head at her own foolishness. "Impossible, of course."

Chris tightened his arm around her. Appreciating the

warmth of his gesture and the nearness of him, she automatically leant her head on his shoulder as she wiped her eyes.

They stayed in that position, without speaking, until her tears had dried up. Chris gave the top of her head a kiss before sliding his arm out from around her shoulders, and standing up.

"A fresh brew, I think." He picked up the mugs. "Stay there, I'll make these."

She watched as he found his way around her kitchen, too numb to insist on helping him. Her mind ran around in circles as she searched for answers. Why would anyone single her house out from a road full of similar houses, all with lovely big gardens? Why would they dig up her plants and shrubs? And as if that wasn't bad enough, why destroy the treasured few belongings she had left from her gran?

Chris put the mugs down on the table, along with a plate of toast.

"Hope you don't mind. I've not long come off my shift, and haven't had breakfast." He sat down next to her instead of his original place on the opposite sofa. "I've made enough for two. Comfort food. I took the liberty of using your bread. Hope that's okay?" He took a slice then pushed the plate nearer to her.

"I always have too much bread and milk in the cupboard these days. I keep forgetting I don't need as much now I'm on my own."

There was a comfortable silence as they drank their coffee and munched the hot buttered toast. Chris had cut it into thick wedges before toasting it. He was right about it being comfort food. By the time the plate was empty, she had calmed down.

She nursed her mug in both hands, taking small sips while different thoughts played and jostled in her head. She let one of them out.

"Chris, have there been any other incidents like this in the area?"

"Haven't heard of any, certainly none that I've had to investigate. Do you think you are being targeted? Did you mention the first intruders to Mike?"

"Yes to both questions. It seems too much of a coincidence for them to be separate incidents now."

"I don't want to worry you, but I agree."

There was a brief silence. Chris studied his hands.

"Do you think its Tony?"

He looked up, straight into her eyes. Was he making sure she told him the truth? Despite his bright blue eyes, there was no hint of coldness, just warmth and caring.

"Truthfully? I don't know. I admit I've wondered whether he would be capable of hurting me in such a way. I'm not sure he would, but even if he was capable, I doubt he could be bothered."

Chris gave her a quizzical look.

"You had to know Tony to understand what I mean. He could be infuriatingly lethargic about any job around the house or outside that involved being physical. If he thought it would impress, he might be seen at the gym on the treadmill perhaps, or jogging along the park in his designer gear… But digging? No."

"Not even for revenge, throwing him out, anger because you caught him out?"

"I suspect not, but who knows? I have doubts about it being him, but who else could it be, with a car similar to his, if I'm the only target?"

"I'm sure Mike and his team will be thorough." He gathered up the mugs and plate, took them through to the sink and rinsed them clean.

She marvelled at this simple act. Tony would never wash a mug, let alone help her with the dishes or laundry; it simply never occurred to him. He would occasionally vacuum and tidy up before she came home from work – but knowing now about his affair with Lucy, she wondered if he did those few things to cover his tracks.

Chris hovered by the sofas before sitting down opposite her.

She started to thank him for washing the dishes at the same moment as he spoke. They both stopped mid-sentence and laughed.

"After you," she said.

"I was about to tell you why I decided to call on you this morning." He paused, took a deep breath, and continued, the words rushing out. "The thing is... I... I get letters and emails periodically, informing me of dance competitions. Usually they go straight into the waste bin, because I don't have a partner, but I wondered... well, I thought..." He cleared his throat. "I thought, if you would like to be my partner for the foxtrot at the next competition, I would fill in the entry form and send it off. I have to submit it by Friday." He gave her a sheepish smile, and crossed over to hand her the print-out of the email. "Please don't feel obliged, but I would love it if you agreed."

She took it from him and had a quick glance at it before putting it down on the table.

"It's a lovely idea, but we won't be eligible for any of the levels. It's a competition for amateurs. Even though you haven't danced in a competition, I'm classed as a professional because I teach, and I danced in competitions as a student. I've already reached a higher level than any of these sections you might class yourself in, and unfortunately the competition rules state you'd have to dance above your level. And I can't dance below mine."

Her heart sank when his eyes, which had sparkled when he asked her to enter the competition, now dulled.

He sighed. "Ah well, it was just a thought."

"There may be a way around it, though. Hang on while I have a look on the internet."

He watched over her shoulder without question, while she keyed in the search on her tablet and waited for it to load.

"There," she said, and pointed to the page. "We are eligible for this competition. It's open to all levels. It's run by the ISDC – Inventive Sequence Dance Competitions – but the date is very close, we'd have to send the form in as soon as possible. Have you ever done any sequence dancing?"

"Not that I'm aware of. Would I notice the difference between sequence and traditional ballroom dancing?" As he spoke, he made a slight frown that disappeared as quickly as it came. "I could learn if there isn't a lot of difference."

"Sequence foxtrot will use the same steps and footwork as traditional, and it's also danced in the 'hold'. The main difference is in the choreography. The sequence routine fits into sixteen bars of music and then repeats. I could show you a few video examples on the internet." She keyed in another search and passed the screen across to him.

He watched for a couple of minutes, and then looked up. "Great! It looks straightforward enough. I'll have a go at that, and I'm free that weekend if you are."

She didn't have to check her diary to know she was free.

"We'll have to practise a lot between now and then, but the answer is yes." She smiled at him and he beamed with genuine delight. "Any special requests for music?"

"Have you got a playlist to choose from? I'm already looking forward to it. We could make a day of it, and after the competition, maybe we could have a meal somewhere?"

"Lovely." She meant it. It had been years since she had entered a competition. She and her partner, a boy six years her junior, had come away with the silver medal. The following year the boy entered with a younger partner from their dance school and won gold. She had been there cheering them on as their tutor.

He sat next to her as they chatted about music and pencilled in days for practising.

"My lounge is too small to use for our final rehearsals, the whole sequence foxtrot will need an area long enough to promenade around in, but it will suffice for the early stages while we choreograph the routine. I could ask Irenka if we can use her studio, at the Wigan dance school, to put it all together."

He looked at his watch, and she guessed what he was thinking. No time like the present.

"Are you in a rush?"

"I do need to get some sleep. I'm usually in bed before lunch when I've been on nights, but I have an hour to spare if you want to run through a few steps now."

He chose *The Way You Make Me Feel* by Michael Jackson

from the foxtrot tracks in her music collection, saying he wanted something more modern than the music his mum had favoured. Privately, she wondered if it was to stop him comparing their dance to his mum's, but she was pleased with his choice.

She plugged her iPod into the speaker dock and placed the remote control in her pocket for when she wanted to pause or rewind the track. Then she set up her tablet with the dancing app, to video their routine.

They danced through the foxtrot steps Chris had danced at the ball, and a tingle of pleasure ran through her as he held her close. The urge to snuggle into his hold was tempting, but she had to make an effort to remember she was supposed to be looking for areas to improve their posture.

"I'll play the video back, to see if it's recorded us properly." She picked it up and pressed a few icons. "I usually hold it to video my students. I've never propped it up to take a selfie video before."

Chris groaned as he watched himself dance.

"Don't worry, the movements only need minor tweaks. Considering you haven't danced for a while, I'm very impressed." She gave him a broad smile. "It could be *me* letting *you* down in this competition."

They watched the video several times, looking for things to improve.

"Right, let's take it from the beginning." She held out her arms to him. "We need to decide which steps to keep and possibly tweak and which to leave out altogether."

Everything went smoothly until Chris took more of an angle on the 'V' step, and they danced into the wall instead of the corner. His warm, firm body, pressed up against hers, making butterflies flutter in her chest, and she gazed up with longing into his eyes. Releasing her from the dance hold he tucked one arm around her waist, leant his other hand on the wall above her head, and bent forward until his lips gently kissed the top of her head, and then her forehead.

Anticipating his mouth traveling down to hers, she tilted her head back slightly but he moved slowly, leaving small kisses in a trail along the bridge of her nose to the tip. She noticed, for the first time, a tiny, almost invisible, scar under his left eye, before letting her eyelids close as she waited for his lips to meet hers. This was the moment she had waited for since the night of the ball, longing to feel his lips on hers again. She arched her back a little so she could accept his kiss and wrapped her arms around the back of his neck.

His lips were warm and as they caressed hers it sent a rush of warm jittery sensations to her chest. His hand behind her waist pulled her in even closer and she was sure she could feel his heart beating. Or was it hers? It was impossible to tell when their bodies seemed to be moulded together. She let herself melt into him, lightheaded with desire. Without his lips leaving hers, his free hand traced her collar bone with the lightest of touches, to the hollow of her throat and down to the top button of her blouse.

She waited for him to undo the buttons, but he didn't. His hand moved slowly over the top of the fabric to cup her breast.

A loud rattle followed by the crunch of gravel from near the front door broke into the moment. As she froze, Chris released his hold on her. With swift reflexes, he shot across the room to the side of the bay window.

Chapter Ten

"Only the postman." He blew out his breath. "I thought it was someone letting themselves into the house!"

"So did I." She inwardly cursed the postman for his bad timing.

"Look at us! We're like naughty school kids, caught in the act." He chuckled, and it was so infectious she found herself joining in. He hugged her tight. "That was a lovely end to a practice session, Gina, and I'd really love to take it further, but not now." He paused and then grinned. "What I mean is, not on this hard floor, and not today. I haven't had any sleep since coming off night shift, and I don't want our first time to be rushed – or on a wooden floor in full view of anyone who comes to your front door."

He released her from the hug and kissed her again, this time only briefly.

"Are you going to be ok when I've gone?" he asked, as he reached the front door. "I'll probably sleep until four o'clock, but if you're anxious or worried or something, text me and I'll reply when I get up. After four you can phone. If there's any sign of more trouble, ring the police immediately. Promise?"

"I'll be fine now. I doubt they'll come back. There's nothing left to smash." In reply to Chris's eyebrow lift, she added, "But I promise."

"Are you at work tonight?"

"Yes. I may go in earlier and choreograph some steps for us, while the studio is empty."

Chris gave her a gentle hug. She wasn't expecting it, and he released her before she could reciprocate.

"Try not to worry too much or let it upset you again, Gina. Next time I have a day off, I'll help you tidy the garden. Then

I'll send our competition entry in as soon as I get home. I'm looking forward to our next practice. I'll phone you later."

A little sense of satisfaction crept over her. He was visibly more relaxed than a few weeks ago. As she waved him off down the path, she realised he'd made his smoothest exit and longest leaving speech since she'd known him.

The next evening she left for the railway station as usual, only to find that they were doing emergency repairs to the line and she had to take the rail replacement bus to Southport, so that she could catch the Wigan train from there. She groaned aloud. It would be a miracle if she wasn't late for the class. The bus was renowned for being snail-slow, winding its way through the side streets to stop at all the stations, but she had no other alternative but to get on it.

It started meandering around the roads, and she gazed through the dusty window. After a few minutes she sat upright when she spotted Chris's silver Peugeot in the drive of a house on the far side of Freshby. The car registration was definitely his, so when he'd walked home with his tool box at the beginning of January, it must have taken him a good half hour.

Funny that they had never spoken about where he lived. He'd always come round to her place, and she'd never thought of asking him. She swivelled her neck as far as it would go, to get a better look at the house. Despite the dark, she could see that the front of the house and the garden were neat. There were lights on in the front room, but the curtains were closed. She made a mental note to look out for the house on her way back. Somehow knowing she was passing his house made her seem closer to him, and it was a comfort, especially as the bus missed her train to Wigan and she had forty minutes to wait until the next one.

She arrived at the dance school almost fifteen minutes late, and to make matters worse, there were signs it was going to be a difficult evening. Her normally amicable boss, Irenka, was in a foul mood, and the atmosphere seemed to affect the mood of the students. She was teaching them new steps to a cha cha dance they'd been learning for over a year. All they had to do was add them after the under arm turn, and before the New York sequence, but they seemed to have become incapable of remembering either, let alone the new steps.

Usually the time flew past when she was teaching, but she found herself looking at the clock twenty minutes before the class was due to finish. The rain was dancing off the pavements as she left the building to walk to the train station. The train was late, meaning her connection with the replacement rail service bus at the other end would be dubious. Could the night get any worse? Everything had been so much easier when she'd used Tony's car to get to work. But any idea of buying and running her own car, on her meagre earnings, was an impossible daydream.

Fortune was stacked against her when she reached Southport, too. Just as she'd suspected, the bus wasn't there. In addition, the main station office was closed, so she had nowhere to shelter out of the rain while she was waiting for it. Her coat was drenched and she could feel the water soaking through her shoes, from the huge puddles lying on the pavements. The deluge was too much for the drains to cope with.

Her hair plastered itself to her face and head, and dripped down the back of her neck, despite having the coat collar up. She was cold and uncomfortable by the time the bus arrived, but even that didn't improve matters, since it had no heating, but blew out a cold draught from under the seats. All she wanted to do was get home, have a hot chocolate and sit right next to the radiator for an hour or two.

On the way along Chris's road she remembered to look out for his house, even though it was difficult to see out of the window. The rain beat against the side of the bus and ran in rivers down the glass on the outside, while her breath and the body heat from other passengers, steamed up the inside windows.

She peered out, squinting to see through the blurred view. She must have missed it. The house she thought was his had a darker car in the drive, but she could have been mistaken. In the dark, through rain-soaked windows, the houses and cars all looked very similar. A loud sigh escaped her lips and she glanced around to see if anyone had noticed. Disappointment took her by surprise. She hadn't realised how much she was looking forward to simply seeing his car in his drive, or his house lights on. He'd also told her he was going on a course in Manchester for a few days so he'd probably already left to get to the hotel, so there would be no point in getting off the bus to walk along the road, find his house and speak to him.

She walked home feeling more alone than she had since Tony left.

The following morning, she picked the envelopes up off the hall floor, riffled through them and sighed. They were all bills. She took them through to the kitchen and threw them on the table, while she prepared a snack. They stared at her throughout her lunch time until she couldn't put off opening them any longer.

She leant on the table with her head in her hands, the opened mail scattered around her. Once more she cursed the postman, but mainly she cursed Tony. She could do with his contribution to the household bills right now.

She'd loaned him a couple of hundred pounds out of her bill money before Christmas to tide him over the festive party weeks. He always went to a dozen or more parties, arguing that it was frowned upon not to join in with socialising, which was also viewed as networking. The run up to Christmas was filled with meals and drinks almost every night. Now, she found herself wondering how many out of those evenings he'd been 'socialising' with Lucy.

Pride stopped her from phoning and asking him to repay the money. No way did she want to give him or Lucy the satisfaction of hearing her begging for the cash, or knowing how difficult she was finding it to pay her bills. He wasn't likely to turn up with the repayment either. Even when they'd still been on good terms, she'd always had to nag him to pay her money back.

However, she couldn't ignore the bills, especially the red one. She had no alternative but to walk into the village and see if there was someone she could speak to at the bank.

If there was a bad day to go to the bank this must be it, she thought, as she walked into the crowded building. The guy who usually hung around the door, like a meet and greet, wasn't there, and there was only one woman at the counter. Nor was there any privacy for asking questions. When it came to her turn, she tried to lean forward so she could talk quietly through the narrow gap in the glass that divided her from the cashier.

"You'll have to speak up love. I can't hear you." The cashier spoke loud enough for everyone to hear. Gina winced inwardly. There were at least half a dozen people in the queue behind her.

"Can I see someone about a loan to pay my bills? Possibly an overdraft?"

"What is it you want? An overdraft or a loan?" the cashier shouted through the division on the counter. "You'll have to speak up. I can't hear you."

At this point Gina wished she could just walk away, but she needed some help to pay her bills, and anyway she didn't want to look rude in front of the queue.

"I want to make an appointment with your financial adviser." She'd raised her voice slightly, hoping it was enough to satisfy the cashier but not enough to entertain the queue.

"He's on holiday. If you need to talk before he comes back in two weeks, you'll have to use the phone over there." She pointed to the wall by the cash machines. "It will put you straight through to Customer Support. Next, please."

Back home, Gina slammed the door and kicked off her shoes. She was burning up inside, positively boiling. She'd never felt so humiliated. How could she ever set foot inside the bank again?

She fought back tears as she made a cup of tea, then as she slammed the fridge door shut, the milk bottle tipped over on the shelf. With a muttered curse, she spent a few minutes on her knees mopping up the milk from the floor and the inside of the fridge. She threw the wet kitchen towels in the bin and placed the milk bottle upright on the shelf. Her tears threatened to start again, until she remembered her gran's favourite phrase: *There's no use crying over spilt milk!* She gave a tremulous smile as all her pent-up anger faded into manageable annoyance.

The phone in her pocket pinged to alert her to a text. It was from Shelley. *Geoff's out tonight. Fancy coming here and cracking open the vino? Any time after eight, if you're free.*

You must be a mind reader, she typed. *Bad day. You may have to prise the bottle from me.* She pressed S*end* and thanked her stars for giving her Shelley as a friend.

She took her mug through to the dining room, where she spent an hour trying to calculate money coming in, and money going out. No matter how many ways she added it all up, she fell short every time.

Shelley had already put the wine in a cooler when Gina arrived. Gina listened to Shelley's tale of the awkward customers they'd had in the shop that morning, whilst sipping from her wine glass.

"What's wrong, Gina? You haven't been listening to me. I know they aren't riveting tales, but it's what my life has become. I have to find my amusement in my customers' habits. You usually see the funny side, but I can see you are somewhere miles away. Spill the beans. Auntie Shelley is all ears." She cupped her hands behind her ears and waggled them.

"Idiot!" Gina was grateful for Shelley's understanding, but as she smiled at her friend, the tears queued up at the corner of her eyes.

"Come on, Gina, I'm acting the clown and you're obviously upset over something. It isn't Chris, is it? I thought things were going well between you two. You know, the 'we have lift off' sort of thing?" She made quotation marks with her fingers.

"It's not Chris. Sorry, Shelley, I shouldn't really have accepted your invite tonight. I'm not in the right mood. I thought at the time it was what I needed, but maybe I just need solitude."

"Nobody tosses Shelley aside in a crisis." She moved her chair closer, filled their glasses, pushed a box of tissues to within Gina's reach, and sat back. "Talk!"

In between sobs and blowing her nose, she told Shelley about her overdue bills and the visit to the bank. Shelley listened, only interrupting with exclamations of "What a cow" and "I'd like to slap her".

"That's the whole humiliating tale. If I'd known they were going to refuse me an overdraft, after making me go through all my incomings and delving into my future freelance finances, I wouldn't have persevered with that phone call in the hearing of everyone in the damned bank, including Paula."

"What?" Shelley gasped.

"Yes. She must have joined the queue while I was talking to the cashier. And of course she heard everything. Not only could I see her constantly smirking, but she even waited for me by the door to tell me to give up teaching dance and find a different job."

"No! Who does she think she is? I hope you told her where to get off?"

"Nope. I scuttled off with my ambitions well and truly down the drain. She took great pleasure in telling me that building up a dance school takes time, experience, and money that I haven't got."

"Don't take any notice of her. She's just jealous and protecting her own territory. She's scared you'll nab her students from under her roof. And you could, Gina. You have a much more approachable nature. She isn't well-liked in Freshby. Respected, yes. Liked?" Shelley shook her head.

"No, she's right. Starting the dance school was my reaction to Tony's infidelity. I didn't think it through enough. I just jumped in on a rebound. My love for all things dance replaced my misplaced love for a two-timing snake." She twirled the remaining inch of wine around the sides of her glass.

"It's just a glitch. Everyone has trouble with bills after Christmas. January is renowned for being miserable where finances are concerned. Phone the companies, ask for extra time to pay. Ask your Wigan school for more hours. You can do this!"

"And this is where I mention that Irenka's also feeling the pinch. I didn't tell you before, and this goes no further, but she's asked me to work fewer hours. I don't blame her, and I could tell she found it difficult to ask me. I'm now doing a third of the hours I used to have, and I think I only still have those because she felt bad. I wouldn't be surprised if she has to let me go within the next month or two."

She watched as Shelley's expression changed from the fiery enthusiasm of the protestor to the despondency of the defeated.

"I wish I could offer you a job, but we only make enough for our needs, plus a little more for treats and holidays." Shelley held up her hand as Gina started to say she wasn't angling for a job. "I know that's not why you told me. I'd take you on like that," she snapped her fingers, "if only I could. We'd have a laugh, you and me." She opened another bottle of wine. "Geoff can do the early shift tomorrow. This is a serious, wine-worthy, double-bottle occasion."

Gina left Shelley's at just before two o'clock and walked home. After many protests from her friend about her safety going home on her own, they agreed taxi money was a waste when it was only a short walk.

A quick text to Shelley, as she locked her door, was met by a speedy reply *Phew. Sleep well. Something will turn up. xx*

Something did turn up.

The police arrived the following morning.

Chapter Eleven

Heavy-eyed and still in her pyjamas, Gina opened the door to two police officers. It had been tempting to stay in bed and ignore the persistent loud knocking, but it was obvious the visitor intended to wait until she answered.

"Gina Pendleton. Can we come in? We have some questions to ask you."

One of the officers was Mike, the policeman who'd called after the vandals had been. He gave her a small but apologetic smile. The other officer looked as though he was in charge. She let them in and motioned them to the sofas in her dining room. She looked out of the door before she closed it. True to form, Mrs Renwick was standing at her bay window.

"Well, *déja vu*," she said lightly as she joined them, but wished she'd thought before saying it. The comment was met with a look of distaste from the officer in charge.

"Do you make a habit of being in trouble with the police, Miss Pendleton?"

"Trouble?" She looked at Mike. "You've come to tell me you found the vandals?" He shook his head, and she looked back at the other officer.

"Can you tell me where you were last night, between the hours of midnight and three in the morning?"

"Yes. I was with my friend, having a drink at her house. She and her husband own the General Store on the main road, and they live above the shop. I got there about eight o'clock. Why? What's happened?"

"What time did you leave the shop and arrive home?"

She told them, and gave the names the officer then asked for.

"I imagine your friend will vouch for you. Did you see

anyone else? Someone who might be able to confirm your leaving and arrival times?"

"My neighbour, Mrs. Renwick is always looking out of her window." She addressed Mike, who was staying quiet and letting the other officer do all the talking. "You already know about her. She probably has some useful information about anything she's seen."

"You didn't see or speak to anyone else?"

She turned her attention back to the officer doing all the talking.

"No. Please, tell me what's going on. Why are you here, if you haven't come about my intruder and vandalism complaint?"

"We've already spoken to Mrs Renwick. We called here earlier, and when you didn't reply, we knocked at your neighbour's house. She saw you leave at quarter to eight. She didn't see you come home, but she did see your boyfriend's car outside your house at about half past two. She presumed he'd dropped you off."

"Chris?" She couldn't think why Chris would be outside her house at that time "But he's on a course in Manchester, with work. He didn't even know I was at Shelley's."

"Not Chris," Mike said. "The car belonged to Anthony Ward. I believe he's your ex."

"Tony? Why would Tony be outside my house at all, never mind at that time? Will you tell me what all this is about?" She was pleading with Mike directly, but it was the other officer who spoke. She realised she didn't know his name, since he hadn't introduced himself. Or had he? Maybe she just didn't notice when she was flustered after opening the door.

"The village dance school was broken into again last night. An eyewitness saw the car, belonging to Anthony Ward, at the scene. They made a note of the registration, because the building alarms were going off. There were goods stolen. Do you mind if we have a look around?" He nodded to Mike.

"Of course not. Although I still don't see why you think I had anything to do with it." The officer didn't reply, but followed Mike out of the room. He returned five minutes later.

"Have you thought about why Anthony Ward would be outside your house?"

"Why don't you ask Tony what he was doing?"

"We have. He denies being there. Said he was with his girlfriend all evening, and you still have the spare key to his car."

Gina was about to protest that she didn't have the key, but at that point Mike returned. The two officers had a quiet conversation out of earshot before the one in charge returned and spoke to her.

"Will you get dressed, please, Miss Pendleton? We have to ask you to accompany us to the station. We can continue this conversation there, where you can make and sign a statement."

In her bedroom she quickly chose a smart, navy blue suit with a straight skirt. The jacket had a stand-up collar so she chose a round neck soft peach blouse to go under it. She reasoned with herself that if she looked smart, they couldn't possibly think she was a criminal, and might treat her kindly. She brushed her hair until it shone. Standing back to check the effect in the mirror, she thought she looked as though she was attending a job interview, not a police grilling.

But why had Tony been outside her house after she arrived home, and why hadn't she heard his car? And why had his car been seen outside the dance school? Had he really been involved in a break-in? And what were the stolen goods?

Putting the last touches to her light make-up, she ran the lipstick over her lips and pressed them together. It had only taken minutes to get ready, but she felt better prepared to be formally interviewed. She walked downstairs to accompany the police to the station.

When she finally arrived back home, Gina sank onto the sofa, tucked her knees up to her chest, and wrapped the fleecy throw around her shoulders. She stayed huddled on the sofa for nearly an hour with her mobile phone held loosely in her hand. Several times she was gripped by the urge to phone Chris, to hear his voice reassure her that everything would be all right. But what could he do? He was on a course, it wasn't his case, and she didn't want to drag him into her mess. She'd tried to keep his name out of everything, but during questioning she couldn't avoid giving him as her alibi for the night of Paula's first break-in.

She tapped the edge of her phone against her lips. Should she phone him? Halfway through tapping his phone number, she thought better of it. He'd find out as soon as he reported back into work.

A shrill tune echoed through the house, and it took her a couple of seconds to recognise that it was her landline phone. Hardly anyone rang her home phone these days. She shifted her feet to the floor, and crossed to the phone.

"Ah, you're home now. I was just checking before I came round to see you. We've had a visit from the police. Don't go anywhere. I'll be at yours in about ten minutes."

True to her word, Shelley arrived at her door bearing a box of cakes and the local morning paper. She followed Gina through to the kitchen, and placed the newspaper, opened at an inside page, on the kitchen table. Gina looked at where Shelley's finger was pointing. There was a paragraph in a small column headed *Crime Update,*

Details are emerging of a second break-in this year, at the hugely successful dance school in Freshby Village. In January the owner, Paula Mellor, reported that silver trophies had been stolen during the burglary at Paula's School of Dance, and the intruders had vandalised the property, causing damage to both the studio and the building.

It is not yet known if the latest break-in is connected to the one in January. We shall add to this update as the details emerge.

"I was reading this, when the police came in to ask me about my whereabouts last night. I tried phoning you several times after they'd gone, but you didn't answer. I wasn't sure if you were ignoring me because you didn't want to talk, or if you'd gone out."

"They took me to the station. It was awful, Shelley. Why would anyone want to frame me?"

"I told them about our CCTV cameras. They show the shop

door and part of the road that leads towards your road. I hope it helps. I let them take the tapes away, but Geoff is now wishing he'd copied them first in case they get lost."

"That's good of you. It seems as though I may need a lot of help. What did they tell you?"

"Not a lot; only the same as what I read in the paper."

"I'll make us a coffee. I can't make any sense of it all, but I think Tony's involved in it somehow."

"Tony?"

She told Shelley everything the police had told her about Tony's car and his response when they interviewed him.

"Surely they don't think you had anything to do with it? The first time Paula's was broken into, you were at a ball with dozens of the local police! If that isn't a cast-iron alibi, what is?"

"You have to look at the bigger picture. That's what they said at the interview. Tony's car has been seen outside mine in the early days after we broke up. Had we really split up or was it just for appearances? The same car was outside the school and then outside mine when the school was broken into for the second time. And – wait for it. They found the stolen trophies in my shed. Not just the ones stolen last night, but also from the night of the ball. They could have been in my shed all this time. I didn't know. They wouldn't believe me that I don't go in the shed in the winter. It only has garden tools in it. It doesn't matter that I had an alibi both times. I could have put Tony up to it, or we could be in it together. And I could be using Chris in his role as a policeman as a way of diverting any suspicion."

"What?" Shelley spluttered, sending coffee over her skirt and the table. She wiped it away with a tissue from her bag. "They think you're only using Chris as a cover? Bloody cheek! I hope you put them straight." Her hand gripped Gina's arm. "What has Chris said?"

"Nothing. I haven't told him anything. I haven't been in touch since he went on the course, and I won't tell him because I don't want to drag him into this. I can't be seen to be doing exactly what they insinuated. Am I making sense,

Shelley? Because I don't understand any of this. It doesn't make any sense to me." Tears trickled down her cheeks but she didn't make any effort to brush them away.

Shelley moved round the table to give her a hug.

"It isn't making any sense to me either. I fail to see why they think you are involved in the actual robbery. Why would you want to vandalise her dance studio? You've been a victim of intruders, too, and stealing her trophies wouldn't benefit you. It won't help in setting up your own classes anyway. They can't think you stupid enough to sell them for the little money you'd get. My money would be on Tony trying to get revenge. Maybe he hopes you'll go crawling back to him when things get tough… Gina?"

Gina heard her friend talking, but she couldn't take any of it in properly. The questions Shelley was asking were the same ones she'd asked herself over and over since the police interview. She ran her tongue between her teeth and lips. Despite the mug of coffee her mouth was dry, and her tears still flowed unchecked. She'd been about to say something to Shelley, but she couldn't remember what it was. Everything was numb. The long drone of buzzing in her ears grew louder.

Shelley rushed to the sink and poured her a glass of water.

"Here, have a sip of this, it's nice and cold. You've gone awfully pale. Go on, drink it, and then rest your head on the table for a while." Shelley grabbed a cushion from the sofa and pushed it along the table.

"What I don't understand," said Shelley, when Gina eventually raised her head again, "is why they are so insistent that you are involved. Why do they think you're the culprit, rather than Tony?"

Gina suddenly remembered what she was going to tell Shelley.

"They found my watch at the scene. It was on the floor in Paula's dance studio."

Chapter Twelve

"When did you last go to that dance school?" Shelley asked. "I didn't know you'd worked there too."

Gina was grateful that Shelley had instantly assumed there was an innocent reason for them finding her watch.

"I've never been inside the building."

"How did your watch get in there then, I wonder? Hang on! How did they know it was your watch?"

"That was easy. There was no great detective work involved in finding that out. It was given to me by my gran, and she had it engraved: *To Gina on your 21st birthday, with love, Gran x*. The clasp was loose, so I haven't worn it for over six months, ever since it fell off when I was shopping in the village."

"Well, that's suspicious. Did you tell the police that? No, don't answer. Stupid question. Of course you did." Shelley shook her head in disbelief at her own questions. "That should prove you're being set up."

"They only have my word for that. I can't prove it." She tucked her hair behind her ear. "Thing is, I kept it in a drawer by my bed. I hadn't even noticed it had gone. It could only be me or Tony who knew it was there. I'm not even certain he knew, because it was on my side of the bed." She untucked her hair from her ear, ran her fingers through the strands and shook it out. "Not only that, but it would mean he took the watch before the Boxing Day party."

Shelley raised her eyebrows in a question and waited for Gina to explain.

"Don't you see? The last time Tony was inside this house was when he was getting ready to go to the party on Boxing Day. Why would he take my watch to the party? If he didn't take it then he must have been carrying around with him while we still lived together. Why? Why would he do that? There are so many unanswered questions."

"Maybe it was in one of his pockets, when you bagged up his clothes."

"You think I didn't go through his pockets first? He often used my bank card to draw cash. I made sure I checked all possible places in his clothes for cash, cards or keys."

"You're right," Shelley agreed. "It's a puzzle."

Gina wished Shelley had been able to stay with her for longer, but Geoff, was eager to get to the wholesalers, and rang to say he needed her back at the shop.

The fingerprinting team arrived soon after Shelley had left. Gina would have appreciated her friend's support through it all, but it seemed typical of the way her day was panning out. Not that they bothered her, they were working outside and around the shed. They'd already taken her prints at the station. No doubt they'd taken Tony's prints too.

For all his faults, she couldn't help thinking Tony wasn't capable of breaking into buildings, stealing goods and setting her up. All for some revenge, for what? Except for finding out about his infidelity and refusing to let him stay in her life, what had she done? Yet he'd lied to the police about her still having his car key.

An hour later there was a hammering at her door. Thinking it was the police again, she answered it. There on her doorstep, as if her thoughts had manifested him, was Tony.

For a few seconds she froze on the spot. She stared at the way his blond hair was sticking out and greasy. He usually washed it each day and styled it neatly; it was his crowning glory. His clothes appeared dishevelled, his eyes tired, and he needed a shave, which was also unusual. She found herself wondering why he hadn't showered, then, as she remembered he'd been questioned by the police before she had, she sprang into action.

She stepped back to close the door, but he was too quick for her and put his foot in the way. He was wearing trainers instead of his usual smart leather brogues, making her think he must have dressed in a hurry. They didn't go with his suit trousers.

"What's the idea then, Gina?" He almost spat her name out. "Trying to stitch me up?"

"Stitch you up? You're the one whose car has been seen at the dance school and outside mine. What have I ever done to you, except lend you money and let you live here on the cheap?" She swallowed and made a quick decision, while on the subject, to ask him for the money he owed her.

"I don't owe you anything!"

"You do. I lent you a couple of hundred pounds before Christmas and I need it for the bills."

"You misunderstand," he said slowly, pronouncing each syllable precisely. "I don't owe you anything! This was never my home. You made sure of that, so why should I pay towards it, or be beholden to you for letting me live here? I didn't exactly live here on the cheap either." He moved closer to her and his voice dropped a tone. "Don't throw that in my face. You had the use of my car. Do you know how much it cost me, filling it up every time you'd been to Wigan and back in it, not to mention the wear and tear?"

He stepped towards her. She backed away, but tripped over her own foot. Instead of falling backwards into the hall, she tried to save herself but somehow managed to twist around and fell sideways onto the door. With her weight against it the door opened fully and banged against the wall. By some miracle she remained upright, but the momentum from her fall meant she was positioned with her back against the door and her feet eighteen inches away.

Tony stepped right in front of her so close she could feel his breath on her face. He hadn't brushed his teeth either. He leant into her, with one hand on the door next to her head. His anger led to him hissing at her through clenched teeth.

"You can forget that money you say you lent me. I had to pay a fortune to have my suits, coats and the rest of my clothes laundered, after the soaking they got in those bin bags. And I have rent to pay." His lips turned up in a sneer. "And she's not as cheap as you, she's classy!"

Gina made an effort to keep from showing how nervous he was making her. Tony had flown off the handle a few times during their years together. She'd learnt to keep her distance. At this close proximity she had to be careful. She changed the subject.

"Why did you tell the police I still have the spare key to your car? You know I sent it back to you. Why try to blame me when the witness saw a man in the car?" It was only then she noticed his car wasn't outside on the road.

"I wasn't the man in the car. I wasn't anywhere near here. Who else has the key to my car but you? I told the police the truth. You never gave it me back. For all I know you and your new boyfriend could have planned this. You could have pinched my car for a few hours, while it was parked on Freshby Lane. The police still have the car too, thanks to you!"

"What about my watch? What made you pinch my watch from the drawer before going to the party? You didn't know we were going to split up that night… Or did you?"

"What are you talking about? What watch?"

She searched his face as he spoke, but he seemed genuinely confused by her question. She didn't pursue it. She didn't want to argue with him anymore. The aggressiveness in his manner seemed to be subsiding. His jawline had softened and his brown eyes were no longer dark and moody. Now, if only he would move out of her way so she could get back indoors, she was sure he wouldn't stop her this time.

Tony gave a deep sigh – a positive sign his temper was cooling down. As he did so, his shoulders moved. It was only a slight movement, but it gave her a clear view past his neck, to the road.

A silver Peugeot was pulling in close to the kerb, slowing to a stop alongside her garden wall. She caught sight of the driver's horrified expression as he glanced over towards them. Before she could attract his attention by shouting or waving, he'd driven forward and completed a three-point turn, between her garden and that of the house opposite.

"No!"

Tony mistook her shout for alarm. Surprised, he

straightened up. He put his hands in the air as if in surrender, then stepped back out of her way.

She pushed herself away from the door and sprinted down the path.

Too late. Chris's car had already reached the bottom of the road and was turning on to the main road out of sight.

Chapter Thirteen

Gina tried phoning Chris again, but it went straight to voicemail. No point leaving another message, since she'd left one the first time she phoned, and he hadn't rung back.

Tony had left as she stood at the gate. He'd pushed past her, mumbling, "I hope I've heard the last of this mess," as if it was all her fault.

She was glad to see him go. She watched him walk as far as four houses down the road before turning back up the path. In the past she'd felt a swell of something akin to pride in her chest at the sight of him going out to work, or returning home in his smart suits. Now, waiting for her phone to ring, she wondered whether it was the clothes or the man she'd fallen for. He was certainly handsome with his clear tanned skin and his gleaming white teeth, but compared to the fluttery way Chris made her feel, Tony was as exciting as a tailor's dummy. His smile seemed to be his one outstanding feature, and because he hadn't used that today, the other side to Tony gave her the shivers. All he was interested in was his image and himself: totally selfish. Lucy was welcome to him. They were well-matched. She wondered how he knew about Chris, unless Lucy had found out and told him.

Thinking of Chris, she tried his number one last time. He didn't reply.

She could understand how it must have looked to him, seeing her with Tony. She would have turned the car around too, if the circumstances had been reversed. All she wanted was the chance to explain.

The door to the dance room was open, so she wandered in and turned on the music. The voice of Michael Jackson singing *The Way You Make Me Feel* played through the speakers. Her instinct was to turn it off, but instead she walked into the middle of the room and closed her eyes. If she tried hard to concentrate on blocking out all the events of the day, she could practise their dance.

She took a long, deep breath in through her nose and let it out slowly through her mouth. It was a technique she used to teach the children, before their medal classes or competitions, to relax their nerves. She moved her shoulders in a circular motion to release the tension, and repeated the breathing three more times.

The song was on repeat, so as the first playing came to an end she took up her pose as if dancing with Chris. The moment the first beat played she stepped backwards, and as she danced imagined his hands firmly guiding her around the floor, their hips close and hands together.

She danced as though the judges were watching. After dancing through the steps to more repeats of the song, she slowly changed to dancing as if there were just her and Chris in the room. If she squeezed her eyes shut, and blocked out everything else, she could conjure him up.

The more she glided smoothly along the floor, the stronger her conviction that she felt the warmth radiate from his body, smelt the sweet herby aroma of his aftershave and relaxed in the strength of his arms. The experience was so vivid that she ached for the real thing.

As she neared the window with her backwards stride, she danced herself into the wall. With her energy sapped, all her focus on dancing disappeared, and she slid down the wall to the floor. She sat there for a long time with her bent knees huddled under her chin, until the light from outside dimmed and left the room, and she was wrapped in the cold, dark, cheerless blanket of loneliness.

A knock at the door brought her out of her vacant thoughts. She looked at the clock. She must have been sitting in that position, staring at the ceiling, for two hours or more. She pushed herself up off the floor and hobbled as best she could, with numb legs and aching back, into the hall.

This time, before she turned the door handle, she put the safety chain across from the door frame. It wasn't a very strong safety device, since it had been loose since her gran had owned the house, but it was a precaution that might hold off an unwelcome visitor for at least a few moments.

She peered through the gap in the open door, then closed it to undo the safety chain and threw the door wide open.

"Come in. You do realise it's not class night, don't you?"

Darren and Dorothy walked past her into the hall.

"Of course. We've come to see you. Are you ok?"

"Darren phoned me, to see if I'd come with him to check on you." Dorothy put her hand on Gina's arm. "I couldn't believe it when he told me what he'd heard."

"I found out some of the information during my tea break at the newspaper office, but on the way home I nipped into the chippy for a Chicken Kung Po and came away with more news than I could get my head around. I phoned Dorothy ..."

"... and I hadn't heard anything. I was blissfully unaware of any goings-on, but when Darren told me and suggested he pick me up I agreed straight away. How are you, my dear?"

She ushered them into the dining room and beckoned to the sofas. "I'll put the kettle on, and then you can tell me what you've heard." She turned towards the kitchen, but Darren put his hands gently on her shoulders and turned her towards the sofa.

"Sit down. I'll make the drinks. You have a nice chat with Dorothy. I'm not good with all this women's heart-to-heart thing, my size nines are far too big to trample sensitively over injured souls."

When they'd gone, the silence in the house was deafening. Darren's over-the-top personality and Dorothy's soothing manner had been a blessing. The fact that they both kept in touch outside the class pleased Gina. It showed how suited they were to dance together. They'd stayed for several drinks, all made by Darren, and he even did the washing up. Although, when he nipped to the loo, Dorothy checked them over to make sure he'd washed them properly.

She was surprised how much they knew of her personal situation, as well as the robbery incident at the other dance school. Word certainly did spread around the village. She'd been embarrassed to hear that news of her trip to the bank had spread, although Darren was probably right in thinking it had been spread by Paula to discredit her. She could see how it might quash her chances of setting up in opposition, if that had been her intention. His other suggestion – that Paula had mentioned her lack of finances to cement the theory that Gina had stolen the trophies for monetary gain – was also a possibility. Either way, it appeared that everyone in the village had their own theory about the robbery.

The biggest surprise to her had been Darren's news that Paula had caught the burglar in the act. Unfortunately, according to the guy at the chippy, who'd heard it from a customer, Paula had only seen the back of the intruder and whoever it was wore a sweatshirt-style hoody with the hood up. When she approached them they'd swung around with their gloved fist and she'd been knocked to the floor. After that the details in the retelling had been many and varied. *Paula had a black eye but otherwise ok, Paula had a broken arm, Paula had a twisted ankle, Paula had a broken foot,* and so on.

If Paula had a vague idea what the burglar looked like, the police would have another line of enquiry to follow. She grasped at the possibility that Paula could be her key to the police catching the real criminals and leaving her alone.

The rest of the evening she spent mulling over all the events of the day and piecing together all the information. Tony didn't wear hoodies. He hated them. '*Wouldn't be seen dead in one*' was a regular quote of his if he saw them in the fashion pages of magazines. But he could have been waiting in the car and had an accomplice. The word '*Why?*' cropped up again and again after every possibility she thought of. When finally she gave up thinking, she checked every window and door lock before climbing the stairs to bed.

The third time she looked at the clock on the bedside table, she got out of bed. It was pointless trying to sleep anymore.

Frustrated with lying awake, she pulled her walking trousers and two fleece tops out of the wardrobe drawer and went to the bathroom to get washed and dressed.

Once out in the chilly dark morning air, her head started to clear slightly. A walk would do her good. *Clear the cobwebs*, as her gran used to say.

Rather than her regular route, where she'd previously come across the aggressive addicts, she chose to walk towards the railway line and golf course. It was still early morning, but she knew by the time she reached the heather fields, many dog walkers would be out on the same trek before their journey to work.

The residential roads along the route were quiet. She was tempted to walk down Chris's road and past his house, but the thought of him being in there, and not being able to speak to him, would be too painful to bear. Instead she walked past the big houses and the small group of thatched cottages, and then turned at the school towards the gorse and heather track.

The wind coming from the coast had a sharp bite to it. Once she was away from the shelter of houses and buildings, she pulled the collar up of her fleece and tied her scarf higher and tighter around her neck. Her thick ribbed pull-on hat covered her ears, keeping them warm.

What a start to a year this was turning out to be! Last year she'd plodded along without a care, blissfully unaware of things happening behind her back. This year her whole life seemed to be like a stage drama, each act revealing a dramatic scenario worse than the one which had gone before.

She was brought out of her thoughts when her foot caught on a raised root in the path and sent her sprawling. The jolt to her foot gave her a painful twinge, and as she bent forwards to rub the area, she heard a movement in the undergrowth. It was too dark to see beyond the front gorse bushes, but even with her hat over her ears she could hear the sound of rustling coming towards her.

"Are you hurt?" A voice at her side startled her; she had been so focused on the rustling movements in front of her. "Do you need a hand to get up?" She looked up at the voice and the proffered hand. As she reached out, the sound of snapping twigs and rapid breathing made her turn her back to the direction of the noise, only to find her face meeting with a long wet tongue.

"Ross! I am so sorry. Ross! Heel! He obviously recognised you from last month." Richard bent down and fixed the lead on the excited Border Collie, before offering his hand to her a second time.

Once she was upright she wiggled her foot and tried putting a little pressure on it. It didn't show any signs of pain, although it was slightly uncomfortable inside her boot. She said as much to Richard, who was looking at her with concern.

"That's a relief! We don't want both dance teachers in the village on crutches."

"Is it true?" she asked him. "Did the intruder hurt Paula? One of my students told me he'd heard she was injured, that she apprehended the burglar." Richard was looking at her. He wore a strange expression. His face had changed from soft and friendly to a more serious, wary one. She leapt in before he could reply. "I suppose you think it was all my doing. That I'm behind the whole thing. The police do. That's probably what the whole village thinks too."

"The police are only doing their job, Gina. They have to take everything into account. It's all evidence, not just fingerprints but statements made of sightings, facts and also hearsay." Even in the dark she could see his face had clouded over. "At the moment, if I'm completely honest, although I am worried about my niece, I am annoyed with her over her accusations towards you. It all had to be recorded. It makes her appear to be a vile person, and adds unnecessary time-wasting work to the job of solving the case and finding the real criminals."

"So you don't think I did it?" She couldn't keep the relief out of voice. "You do know something of mine was found at the scene, don't you?"

"I've worked long enough in the police, my dear, to know when something was planted to throw suspicion on someone innocent. This is why I'm angry with Paula. She's accused you of stealing the trophies to use as display if you set up a dance school. They weren't engraved with the school name; most were just engraved with '1st' then the rest engraved with the name of a dance, like latin, foxtrot and jive for instance. I think she was jealous of your foxtrot with our Chris. In pointing the finger at you, she has also put herself in the spotlight."

"I don't understand."

"By taking the opportunity to have a go at you, she has put herself in the position of having a motive to raid her own school, and then try to make it look as though you did it!"

"No, I didn't mean that. What I really don't understand is why she felt the need to accuse me in the first place. She knows I'm not a threat. She was in the bank when I had to tell them my sorry tale about being short of money, and although I didn't like the advice she gave me at the time, she was right. I'm going to look for another job. A proper job, full-time and everything, not just snatching the few freelance hours available here and there."

Richard sighed. "I love my niece, Gina, but I don't profess to understand her. Why she does a lot of things is a mystery to me." He gave his dog a treat and stroked his head, muttering "Good boy," then turned back to her. "You might need to rest that foot. My car is outside the school. Walk back with me and I'll run you home. No point putting more pressure on it when you need it for dancing."

They reached Richard's car just as huge spots of rain slowly dropped on them. He chose the route she'd decided against when she left the house a few hours ago, which would take them past Chris's house. By the time they reached his road, the deluge of rain was making the wipers swing with speed across the windscreen. Unlike the bus journey, though, she could see through the window and spotted Chris's car in the drive. The lights were on in the front rooms of the bungalow. He must be getting ready for his shift, she thought, as she checked the time on her phone. It was six-thirty, he would be in work at seven. If he was going to phone her today it would probably be in the evening.

Rather than sit in all day waiting to see if he got in touch, she would go into the village and look for a job. Provided, of course, that people there still trusted her.

"Don't worry about what the people in the village think, Gina," said Richard, as if reading her thoughts. "They love a bit of gossip, but you'll be old news by the end of the week."

As she stood outside her front door, about to unlock it, she could hear the phone ringing and fumbled with the key in the lock.

"Please keep ringing. Please keep ringing." She said over and over. Eventually she flung the door open and ran to the phone. She glanced at the time on the phone as she picked it up. Not yet seven o'clock. It could be Chris. She picked it up.

"Hello?"

Chapter Fourteen

"Gina! Thank goodness you're at home. I've tried phoning you since six, but you weren't picking up either phones. Is there any chance you can come in and cover for us? I need to take Geoff to Accident and Emergency."

Disappointment washed over her that it wasn't Chris, but there was no time to dwell on that. Her friend needed her.

"Of course. See you in ten minutes."

She rushed to change into better clothes and grab her mobile, then sprinted to the shop. Geoff's usually ruddy complexion was a pale grey tinged with yellow. He had a large cut on his head that ran with blood each time he lifted the paper towels off it to change them for clean ones. He was sitting on a chair by the door and unusually quiet.

"Go on, Shelley, I'm here now. Get Geoff to the hospital. You can tell me the story of how it happened when you get back." She chased Shelley from behind the counter and waved them off.

She organised the newspaper boys, tidied the rest of the newspapers on the shelf and served the early-morning customers. To her dismay, one of the work-suited men who came in for a newspaper made a snide remark to her, saying he "hoped Geoff had checked his stock before leaving her in charge".

"Don't take any notice of him," said the elderly lady, as she put her bottle of milk and loaf on the counter. "I heard he lost in court to his wife yesterday. She got the house, custody of the children and a chunk of his pension. He's just feeling bitter against women."

Wow, thought Gina. Richard was right; the village loves its gossip. My news will soon be old news. She was relieved that someone else was now the subject of their interest, and replied, "No wonder he's feeling sore. It's always difficult when there are children involved."

A murmur of agreement emanated from the people in the queue. Young and old joined in the discussion about rights and relationships. Gina listened to all of them, occasionally reaching to take the money from people in a rush to get to work.

By the time the group had dispersed, she found that the huge weight she'd carried around since the previous day had lifted. Once the subject had moved away from the original man who'd made the biting comment, she realised everyone had much more interesting things to think about than anything she was, or wasn't, supposed to have done.

Shelley returned with Geoff at lunchtime. Geoff went straight through to the back to lie down, but Shelley took off her coat and took up her normal position behind the counter.

"Sorry we were so long. We waited ages to be called and then they X-rayed him and stitched him up. He doesn't do hospitals. He kept feeling faint and went all wobbly on me. Men, eh! Maybe next time he lifts a heavy box off the top shelf he'll use both hands. That way it won't slip and fall on the floor, clonking him on the head on its way down."

Shelley broke off with a laugh before continuing, "Seriously though, I did get a shock. He's a useless daft lump at times, but I love the whole bulk of him. Seeing him on the floor, out cold, with blood pouring from his head, I panicked. I should have closed the shop and phoned for the ambulance, but all I could think of was getting hold of you to cover here, while I took him to the hospital myself. I didn't want to let him out of my sight. Stupid, isn't it? Luckily he started coming around and once I helped him sit up, he was starting to look a bit less like death." Shelley stopped to catch her breath.

"It seems to me you could do with a drink. I'll go and put the kettle on. You've had a shock." Gina dragged the chair to behind the counter and pushed it towards Shelley, insisting she sit on it. "I'll make one for the invalid too."

She took the drink through to Geoff, who was sprawled on

the couch.

"Thanks love, you're a star," he said, propping himself up to take a sip. "Perfect! Just what the doc ordered. Chris has found a good-un in you."

"I'm not sure he thinks that at the moment. Probably thinks the opposite, in fact."

"What's wrong? Thought Shelley said you two were getting on brilliantly?"

"It's this burglary thing. Tony came around to have a go at me over it all, Chris saw us, and now won't answer his phone to let me explain."

"I'm sure he will eventually, love. He's bowled over with you. He'll not keep away for long, you'll see. Trust your Uncle Geoff." He gave her an exaggerated wink, and winced as it hurt his head.

She smiled to herself as she closed the lounge door. Both Shelley and Geoff had the same habit of exaggerating winking. They were made for each other. She hoped Geoff was right about Chris. Maybe she would try phoning him again, one last time, after his shift ended.

Determined to go into the village to search for a job, she grabbed a quick snack when she got home, and ran herself a hot bath. As a treat, she added an expensive bubble bath Irenka had bought her for Christmas. It had the aroma of a country garden and soaking in the water full of bubbles, with her eyes closed, was so relaxing she didn't want to get out. When the water cooled down she quickly soaped and rinsed her body, and used the shower hose to wash her hair.

Choosing a third set of clothes for that day, a smart pale blue top and navy trousers, she looked at her reflection in the bedroom mirror and tidied a stray bit of hair. The rain had stopped, but from the way the trees were moving she could tell there was still a breeze. Should she tie her hair back to keep it tidy, or take a chance on the weather and leave it down? She settled on leaving it down, it framed her face well making her look as though she'd made the effort to be fit for an interview.

The list of places in the village with vacancies lay on the hall table. She checked the time. If they stayed open until five-thirty she had about three hours to get around them all. Unsure whether to spray perfume or not, since some of the places on the list served food and she wondered if it would be frowned on, she decided against it and reached for her coat from off the banister.

With her house keys between her teeth, she shoved an arm in her coat sleeve. At the same time as struggling to get her other arm in the remaining sleeve, she opened the front door.

What she saw on the doorstep made her gasp. Her keys fell to the floor and she stood transfixed with her mouth open. Standing there poised to knock at the door, was someone with the most enormous bouquet of cream and dark peach roses, soft pink peonies, warm pink carnations and white chrysanthemums. She glanced past the flowers to see if the florist van was parked outside, and got an even bigger shock when the bouquet was lowered revealing no other than Chris.

"Chris! I thought you'd be at work! What—?"

"I am so sorry. I'm a complete and utter idiot. Forgive me, please? I've been acting like a jealous teenager." He handed over the flowers and stepped past her into the hall.

"They're beautiful. They must have cost a fortune." She closed the door and walked through to the kitchen to put them in the sink. Chris followed her.

"It's only money. I nearly lost something worth much more than a bunch of flowers. I thought I'd surprise you on my way home from Manchester. When I saw Tony leaning over you in the doorway, I was furious. I thought to myself, 'I've only been away four days and she gets back with her ex' – only I thought much stronger words than that, you can imagine! I went home and seethed. I should have answered your calls and let you explain, but I was too stubborn. Didn't want to appear soft and a pushover, I suppose." He put his hand up to stop her from commenting. "Then this morning – well – I'd hardly got through the doors at the station before they began asking me if I'd spoken to you since yesterday. When they discovered I didn't have a clue about everything that's gone on, they couldn't wait to fill me in on the news."

He put his hands on her shoulders and pulled her in against

his chest. With his arms wrapped around her, she snuggled in and listened to his heartbeat. He kissed the top of her head.

"I was going to call around this evening, but all morning the thought that Tony could have been threatening you, and I did nothing about it, gnawed away at me. In the end I got Terry in to cover for me and left early. Why was Tony here? Was he being threatening?"

"He was angry, certainly. Not very nice at all, but he thought I'd set him up somehow. It's a puzzle. I don't know whether to believe him. I know I didn't do anything, but I can't stop being upset by it all. I'll be glad when they solve it. Are you on the team investigating it?"

"No. Even if they needed extra officers, I couldn't be on it, because I'm involved with you. If it's any consolation, though, I did discover that they didn't find any fingerprints at the dance school or here. What they did find, however, is prints from the soles of shoes around your shed and in some of the building dust at the scene. All men's shoe prints."

"Men's?"

"Two different prints, size nine and ten, so two men." He hugged her tighter. "Don't worry, we'll catch them"

He brought his head down to kiss the top of her head again, and then tilted her chin upwards so he could carry on kissing down her face. Remembering when they'd kissed after the ball, she closed her eyes and waited for his warm lips meeting hers. He gently kissed the tip of her nose, and her cheek, and then buried his head in her hair and inhaled. She heard him moan slightly as he ran his fingers through her hair.

Every nerve in her body tingled as she waited for his lips to meet hers. His aftershave teased her senses with subtle wafts of lemon thyme and patchouli. His chin's slight stubble rubbed against her cheek. He gave a deep sigh of pleasure and said softly, "I've missed you so much these past few days." Then his lips met hers, kissing her with such urgency and longing, that she was left in no doubt precisely how much he'd missed her.

Her head was spinning when their lips eventually parted, and she was sure she'd forgotten to breathe, so engrossed was she in this kiss.

"I've been thinking of being with you ever since the postman interrupted us. I imagined us dancing again, and I would lead you into the wall so we could finish where we left off." He gave her a mischievous smile. "I'm not sure I can wait long enough to reach that part of the dance, and I'm certain a bed would be more comfy than a solid wooden floor." While he waited for her response, he held the back of her head and ran soft kisses along her neck. "Your hair smells lovely, and feels so silken, it has that just-washed— I stopped you from going out, didn't I? Were you going somewhere important?" He leant back to look at her face.

"Nowhere that can't wait until tomorrow." She hadn't wanted him to stop. Her body ached for him to hold her and run some more kisses along her skin again.

"Then shall we continue upstairs?" He tilted his head to one side as he spoke.

The heat burned in her cheeks and she thanked luck for prompting her to have a bath. She smiled at him self-consciously, and gave a little happy huff of breath and a few quick nods of her head in approval.

"I just need to make a quick phone call, if you don't mind? In case I forget to make the call later. Best do it while it's on my mind now. I'll follow you up." He raised his eyebrows in question, and when she nodded gave her a quick kiss before he went outside to dial.

She didn't ask him who he was phoning or why; it was none of her business. She took her coat off and hung it back on the bannister. Upstairs she hurriedly straightened the duvet and flung some of her worn clothes in the linen bin. She brushed and smoothed her hair and as she checked her teeth in the mirror, he appeared behind her, slipping his arms around her waist and placing his chin on her shoulder.

"Caught you! Stop checking the mirror. You look beautiful as you are." He turned his head slightly to plant a kiss on her cheek, all the while keeping his gaze on their reflection.

The intense look in his deep blue eyes sent all her senses into disarray. She turned around in his arms to face him, hoping for another long lingering kiss.

Her arms were around his neck, he tasted of mint, and she could feel his breath on her cheek becoming more urgent the longer they kissed. Eventually he released her, and taking her arms from his neck, he held her hands in his and walked slowly backwards, bringing her to the side of the bed.

There he guided her hands to the buttons on his shirt, helping her to undo the first one, and leaving her to undo the rest as he emptied his trouser pocket of a packet of mints and another small packet, placing them on her bedside table.

"I popped in the chemist, in the hope…"

She stopped him talking by planting her lips on his, while her hands, finished with undoing buttons, moved to his belt. He untucked the shirt from his waistband and slipped it from his shoulders, revealing olive skin and firm muscles, before tossing it onto the floor. His belt undone, he lifted her arms to slide her top over her head. She sighed as he ran his hands through her hair to untangle it. His hands didn't stop at her hair, and warm ripples of pleasure cascaded over her as he caressed her skin, all the while his lips lay a slow trail of light kisses to her breasts.

Chapter Fifteen

Gina could hear the gentle sound of Chris's breathing, and the rhythmic beat of his heart as her head rested on his chest. His arm lay protectively over her as he slept. It was dark in the room: the light outside had disappeared long ago.

Their legs were entwined still, from where she'd snuggled in to him before they both drifted off to sleep. Her ankle ached a little from being in the same position, but she didn't want to move it and wake him up. She was making the most of being next to him

She detected a slight movement and realised that he was watching her.

"Hi." She tilted her head further to look up at him.

"Hi. You been awake long?" He pulled her closer, ruffled her hair and hugged her tightly as he yawned. "What time is it?"

"Not sure, but I feel as though I've slept for hours."

His chest moved from under her cheek as he wriggled into a position from where he could reach his watch on the bedside table.

"Seven-thirty! We *have* been here for hours. Sorry I didn't keep you awake for most of it."

She giggled. "Oh, I'm fairly sure we were wide awake for all the afternoon. Time just ran away from us. It does that when you are enjoying yourself." She felt the heat rise in her face. It was a good job the room was dark.

He chuckled. "Mmm, it was rather special, wasn't it? I'd love to say let's do it all again, but that'll have to wait until another day, I'm afraid." He moved his arm, so she raised her shoulders, and let him rescue it. "Sorry, pins and needles!" He shook it, opened and closed his fingers a few times, and sat up. "I hate to say this, because I know it's not very romantic, but I'm starving. I haven't eaten since breakfast. I could nip to the chippy, if you fancy something off their menu?"

"I'm peckish too, but not for a big meal. I could rustle up something on toast?"

She wrapped her dressing gown around her and tied the belt. He'd agreed to having a snack; now she hoped there was enough cheese to go on the toast. Maybe she should have let him buy a take-away after all.

He flicked the bedside lamp on, and stood up. She couldn't help but look at his lean, well-toned body as he stretched first, and then reached for his clothes. He caught her looking and smiled. His brown hair, even more tousled than usual, made him look younger and impish.

By the time he reached the kitchen, she'd made the cheese on toast and mugs of tea, and placed them on the table. She motioned for him to sit down. Worried that it didn't look much to give him to eat, she looked through the cupboards for something else.

"Everything okay?" he asked.

She turned to answer him and saw he had the final demand bill in front of him. He nodded towards it, which she presumed meant he was asking about her bill.

"Yes, fine!" she said, slightly sharper than she intended. She didn't want to spoil the moment. If she'd noticed it first, she would have cleared it away before he came down. It was her fault for leaving it lying around. She reached to move it from the table and he caught her hand.

"I'm not criticising or being nosy," he said softly. "I want to help, if you'll let me. I could give you the money, tide you over?"

"Don't be daft. I can't take your money!" She gave a small sigh. "Well, not unless you were planning to be my new lodger?"

Chris laughed, but didn't answer her question.

"Is that the reason you're struggling? Is the lack of Tony's money towards the house bills a problem?"

She sat down to eat her toast, but she'd barely lifted it to her mouth when she realised he was still watching her, and would carry on waiting for an answer. She sighed, put her toast back on the plate, and told him all about the bank and about Tony, not only owing her rent but also not paying her the loan back either.

"That's all he paid you towards the house each month? He was lucky, I pay more than double that for my house, and that doesn't even cover my council tax and utilities. Yet he messed around paying it and still asked for loans too?"

Chris's eyes narrowed, and with his jaw clenched, looked for one minute as if he was going to bang on the table with his fist, but instead he blew out a breath and shook his head.

"I'm sorry, Gina, but I can't abide men like that, taking advantage of a woman. Whether in relationships, or the likes of workmen conning women living on their own, it really winds me up."

She was thankful she hadn't mentioned Tony borrowing from her each month. Instead, nodding towards the bill, she said, "It proves how much I needed that little extra though. I start a job search tomorrow. My freelance teaching has been cut too."

"Oh, Gina!" Chris moved around to her side of the table to give her a hug. "I have six days off from the day after tomorrow. If you haven't found a job by then, I could help you with your search. Drive you around or something? I really want to help you."

"Thanks, but hopefully one of the places on my list will take me on. Then maybe we could use one of your days as a Valentine's Day outing."

"I'd like that, good idea. In the meantime, I'd best be going. I've work in the morning and I might just grab some chips on the way home." He gave her a cheeky smile. "I need to replace the calories I worked off this afternoon!"

She chuckled. "Save some energy for our foxtrot rehearsals. I'm working tomorrow night, but we should get back to our rehearsing."

"Day after tomorrow, I promise. I'll be in touch." He pulled his keys from his pocket and jiggled them in his hand. "Right now, the chips are calling."

He gave her a tight hug and a long lingering kiss, and strode down the hall and out of the door.

She sat at the table with several of the local papers open at the S*ituations Vacant* pages. It was too early to go to bed, and she'd already arranged the beautiful flowers he'd bought, in three of her gran's vases, and taken photos of them. Never before had she received a bouquet as big and expensive as that. Even the bouquets for winning competitions had been smaller than the collection of flowers in just one of her vases.

Looking through the papers proved to be a waste of time, so she gathered them up and took them out to the recycle bin. It was only when she cleared the table of their snack dishes before going to bed that she noticed the final demand was missing. It wasn't in the kitchen. She concluded that she must have put it out with the newspapers and made a mental note to look in the morning.

True to his word, Chris phoned her the next evening after she got back from Wigan. She'd wanted to sound upbeat but when she heard his voice all she could say was, "I wish you were here right now. I could do with a hug."

"What's wrong? Didn't the job hunting go well?"

"That was one reason, and to top the day, it was my last class at Wigan tonight, although I didn't know that until the class was over. Irenka had a word with me after everyone had left. She paid me for tonight's class, and told me she was sorry to see me go. I didn't get to say goodbye to the students either. When she reduced my hours, she led me to believe I'd be there for at least a few months more. It was so sudden."

She'd hoped Chris would say he'd come around to cheer her up, but he didn't.

"Oh, love, don't get down, something will crop up soon, I'm sure. I'll come to yours tomorrow morning. I've been looking forward to these days off. We can either job-hunt for you, go for a walk, or foxtrot. I'll bring a hug or two with me."

By the next morning, she'd forgotten her disappointment in

Chris not charging around, like some white knight, to rescue her from the doldrums. It had, after all, been eleven-thirty when she finally hung up the phone, and he'd been at work since early that morning.

The longing to see him had intensified overnight, and she'd woken several times to look at the clock, just in case she overslept. When he finally knocked at the door, she was host to a kaleidoscope of butterflies gathering force in her stomach and tremors running down her spine, to the point where she flung herself into his arms as soon as she'd opened the door.

"You don't know how pleased I am to see you!"

"I think this is a clue," he said. His face lit up as he laughed and he hugged her tight. "If you just let me over the doorstep, I will show you how pleased I am to know how pleased you are to see me."

Once in the hall, he closed the door and placed his warm soft lips on hers. She surrendered to his kiss.

It would have been easy for her to guide him upstairs and lie in his arms again, but during the phone call the previous night, they'd decided to use the time to dance through their foxtrot. While she switched on the music, Chris went through to the kitchen to make them coffee. *The Way You Make Me Feel* played over the speakers and she heard him singing along loudly, above the sound of the kettle boiling.

How did I get so lucky? she thought, as she listened to him. He'd found his way easily around her kitchen and, unlike Tony, thought of her needs as well as his own. They drank as they talked through the steps and various figures to match the music.

The length of the floor in her room was proving to be a real problem for a decent rehearsal. Chris had long legs, giving him a lengthy stride. His long smooth step forward, coming straight from the hip, needed space. She knew she could match his steps, but in her room five of his long walk steps brought them to a halt at the bay window two steps short of the opening to the feather-step followed by the telemark. Each time they had to rush back to the opposite wall to carry on where they left off. At first, they found it hilarious. The foxtrot practice became a mix of working on their natural twist turns, reverse turns and impetus turns, interspersed with laughter stopping their flow, then they'd snatch a hug or kiss, before trying the steps again. The laughter soon wore off, when after an hour and a half of stops and starts, it was obvious that space was a huge problem if they intended to compete seriously.

Her original plan to use the studio in Wigan was no longer a viable one. Irenka had made it quite clear that not only was she no longer needed to teach, but all ties to the school or students should be severed. Probably to make sure she didn't try to encourage Irenka's students to follow her to her own or another dance school.

Short of hiring a church hall for their dancing practice, she was at a loss where else to go. She voiced what they'd both been thinking, that they needed a bigger place to rehearse or they wouldn't be good enough for a competition.

"Let's take a break. We could drive into the village for some lunch, and then if we have an idea for somewhere with space, we'll have the car with us to go and check it out."

Chris came up with an idea as they tucked into baked potatoes with cheese and tuna in the Potting Shed Café.

"I'm not telling you what it is. You'll think me mad, but bear with me. We can go when we've finished here." He gave her the cheeky grin that excited her, and set all her senses tingling. She smiled along with him.

"Sounds very mysterious. Will I like it, or are you not telling me now because you think I'll balk at it, and refuse to go?"

"Wait and see."

"You *are* mad!"

Chris laughed, and switched off the engine. He'd driven down the car track past the woods, to the car park near the start of the dunes. He turned to her and swept his arm the width of the windscreen.

"The car park's empty. There's no-one around yet. Plenty of

space. What more could we want?"

"Thermal underwear?"

They both laughed as she followed him from the car to the centre of the sandy, gravely surfaced area, and surveyed the ground.

"Not that smooth, but not as full of potholes as I'd imagined either," Chris said, as he moved loose stones with his shoes. "Some areas are better than others. It could work as a temporary measure."

He took hold of her, and guided her to a flattish area, and then bowed and held out his arms for her to join him in a dance. He hummed Michael Jackson's song as they completed a circuit of foxtrot, without stopping, and miraculously without stumbling on the uneven bits of ground.

"Not bad!" she said. "Of course this is only handy for the daytime practice, but it certainly makes a difference to our strides and posture. I can see, just from this rough dance-through, that it flows well. Not such a mad idea after all, Chris."

"I don't fancy being a Gene Kelly, dancing in the rain, though. We can't use it in the dark, and I can't skim the floor with the ball of my foot properly to get it smooth flowing and continuous, but you're right. It gave us an idea of how the whole dance fits together." He balanced on one leg while he took off his shoe to shake some grit out of it. "The right footgear would certainly improve my steps too. A few more trials?"

They spent another hour on the whole foxtrot sequence, during which she spent the majority of it visualising them both dancing on a beach in the sunset. Not the Freshby beach, but one on the coast of Italy, just her and Chris with the rest of their married life ahead of them.

"Shall we call it a day?" His voice brought her out of her daydream. "Let's go for a walk, while we're here. It'll be getting dark soon, and it's a shame to waste the opportunity of a walk on a dry day."

She took the hand he offered, and they walked over the dunes, away from the sea, towards the asparagus fields. The trees here were stunted, and oddly-shaped, from the wind coming off the sea. It always reminded her of the *The Lord of the Rings* books. The coast was such a diverse and varied landscape of man and nature that she never tired of walking through it.

He helped her over and through the mud and puddles lying in the narrow gap between two angled posts, meant to keep the motorcycles out of the woods. He was still holding her when she voiced a plan that had hatched in one of her waking moments during the night.

"I thought we could go out for Valentine's Day. Now that I'm unemployed and you're off work, we could make a whole day of it. Take the train over to the Wirral, maybe West Kirby or Parkgate, then head back to Liverpool for a meal. There's a lovely Italian restaurant by the bombed-out church, maybe book tickets to see Bren Rourke. He's on at the small theatre there."

"I'd love to, Gina, but I'm afraid I can't do the evening. We could still go to the Wirral and have lunch, though."

Her chest tightened. That didn't seem right, but he wouldn't lie to her, surely? Only yesterday he was saying how pleased he was at having some days off work.

"Oh! I thought you said you were off for a few days?"

She noticed him look to his feet, a sure sign that he was uneasy.

"But that's it, Gina, I only have the days off, so not Valentine's night, I'm afraid. We can fit in quite a bit during the day though."

He hadn't quite answered her question, but, reluctant to challenge him, she let it pass.

The path became single track for the next half mile so Chris led the way. It wasn't easy to talk as they walked along a very uneven, damp and narrow gap between the shrubs and brambles. Her concentration focused on avoiding the wettest bits of ground and tree roots as they approached the area where the path became slightly wider.

It was during the lull in conversation that she heard the unmistakeable sound of someone moving in the bushes between the trees. Instead of alerting Chris to the sound, she turned to face it.

She opened her mouth to scream as a figure lunged towards her.

Chapter Sixteen

The scream didn't materialise, but the loud grunt from her breath escaping in the shock of contact with the ground, did.

Chris spun around, concern clearly engraved on his face.

"Gina! Are you ok?" He bent over, reaching out to help her to her feet.

"I'm fine. But that guy," she pointed to behind her and a man wearing a hoody, sprinting away down the track, "I've seen him before."

Chris gave chase. She watched as he sprinted after the man, his long legs closing the gap, until he ran out of her sight.

She was sure the man was part of the group that had harassed her in January, when she'd walked along the other path to the dunes. Also going through her head was some gut instinct that he could be involved, somehow, in the vandalism of her garden and the robbery at the dance school. She couldn't describe why she had the feeling he was involved; all she knew was her stomach was churning and she felt sick at the thought. Of course, she might be judging him just because he was wearing a hoody.

Luckily for her, she'd fallen at the side of the track. When she checked, her trousers and jacket were just dusty from the weeds and sand, but nothing that a good brush down wouldn't mend. She hoped she wasn't making a habit of falling over on her walks. In all the years she'd walked along the coastal way at Freshby, she'd stayed on her feet, and then twice in two months she'd fallen over.

"He got away." Chris gave a huge sigh. "I should have anticipated him leaving the path, but I wasn't on the ball. He dived into a dense clump of tall shrubs and trees and I lost sight of him." He put his arms around her shoulders and gently nursed her to his chest. "You say you've seen him before. When? At your house? Do you think he was the one looking in at the window?"

"I never thought of that. He could have been, I suppose. No, he was part of a group that hassled me a few weeks ago." She told him of her meeting with Richard and Ross, the Border Collie.

"Nice guy, Richard. I've a lot of respect for him. Wonder why the bloke jumped out at you? Maybe he recognised you and thought you'd come looking for him." Chris must have noticed that his statement caused her some alarm, because he backtracked. "A bit of a wild theory though. Probably just high on drugs and he was startled by us."

She hoped Chris was right. She couldn't bear the thought of the man recognising her; it was much better to think it a coincidence.

Chris released her and looked around, stooping to peer through the brambles and shrubs.

"Which direction did he come from, your side or from behind?"

"From the side, there." She pointed to the spot from which she'd seen him lunge.

Chris unbuttoned the hood from his coat and wrapped it around his hand for protection. He pushed the brambles back, bit by bit, to make his way into the thicket. He hadn't gone more than five or six yards when she heard him exclaim, "Ah!" He rejoined her on the path and pulled out his mobile phone, and she caught most of the conversation as he had to practically shout and repeat words. There was always a bad signal along the coastal route.

"Terry. Are you anywhere near Gore Lane? Great. Well, I'm on Fisherman's Path. There's an interesting haul here, you may want to come and bag it up, take photos and such like. Some residents are going to be happily reunited with their valuables." He gave Terry more specific instructions and made his way carefully back through the brambles.

"We'll have to wait here. You don't mind do you?"

He wrapped his arms around her and she sank her head into

his chest. She didn't mind being anywhere in the cold, if she could be this close to Chris. His aftershave blended with the fresh scent of wild herbs and shrubs hanging in the air around them, and the warmth radiating from his body tugged at her emotions. She could lose herself in Chris; just being next to him set her heart pounding. With his arms around her protectively she felt very secure.

Terry and Mike, the officer she'd met before, arrived within the hour.

"You had to choose the worst location in this part of the dunes, didn't you Chris? It's taken us over half an hour to reach you from where we parked up." Terry nodded at Gina to acknowledge her, but turned back almost instantly to talk to Chris.

Mike smiled briefly. "It didn't help that we got lost a few times."

Terry scowled and glared at Mike before addressing Chris. "So this is where you two go for privacy! No wonder I hadn't clocked you with her before. I hate this place, it's all trees, greenery, mud and sand. Look at the mess I've made on my shoes. Give me a pub with a beer garden and big-screen TV any day. So, anyway, where's this loot you found?"

Chris laughed. "You're going to love this. It's six yards in that direction." He pointed straight ahead. "Through all this greenery you love so much. Careful!" He was too late warning Terry, who'd already discovered he couldn't simply move the brambles aside with his bare hands and was now swearing profusely. Chris passed Terry his hood to wrap his hands, at the same time that Mike dragged some gloves out of his pocket. Terry sucked at the hand that was now scratched and bleeding, waved aside the offer of Chris's hood, and motioned for Mike to forge ahead through the brambles instead. Still swearing, Terry followed.

Chris left Gina standing on the path to go and chat quietly with the two officers. She could see them nodding heads and using their hands to talk, but she couldn't hear the conversation. Probably police stuff; no doubt Chris would tell her if it was important. The three men stood in a group, heads down, looking at the valuables. Terry broke off a long twig and poked at them. Chris said something, then, tapping Mike on the elbow, he turned to face her and walked back.

"Right, we can go back to the car. They don't need us anymore. They'll sort it here and I'll nip in the station on my way home from yours. By the looks of the amount of jewellery, wallets and other stuff in that hole, there will be some long hours spent searching through files of stolen goods. It could take them days."

On the walk back to the car, she started at every snapping branch and rustle from the wind around them. Why hadn't she noticed these unsettling sounds before? Usually on walks, she noticed the sounds of the birds, or the slight scratchings of the red squirrels running up tree trunks or along branches. She was thankful for having Chris's hand to hold, although she noticed that he was more watchful, too. She'd caught his head turn quickly at a cracking sound more than once.

Chris was quiet in the car on the way home, although he smiled at her several times whilst driving, so it was a comfortable silence. She didn't feel the need to talk either; she was just enjoying being in his company. She was brought out of her reverie when he suddenly turned the car into a parking place in front of a row of shops, and switched off the engine.

"Fancy a Chinese? They do English as well if you don't." He led the way into the restaurant, found them a seat in the corner, and passed her the menu. "I hope you're hungry. All that walking has given me an appetite."

"Hello, Mr Jackson, we haven't seen you for a while. We thought you'd found somewhere else to go."

"I've been busy, Manchu."

Manchu, a small man in his sixties, nodded at Gina. "I can see that!" He neatened his bow tie, gave her a broad smile and bowed slightly. "Have you made your choices? Mr Jackson, can I get you your usual?"

They ordered a combination of Salt and Pepper Mushrooms, Skewered Chicken with Cantonese sauce, Sizzling Fillet Steak in a wine sauce, and Chris's favourite of Pak Far Duck served with chips and rice.

"That seems an awful lot of food for a normal weeknight." Gina spoke in a low voice so the staff couldn't hear her.

Chris laughed. "I'm not trying to impress you, if that's what you're thinking. What we don't finish I'll take home. It will do for a snack." He stopped talking as the first course was brought over and placed on a plate warmer in front of them.

"Thanks Manchu. Manchu?"

"Yes, Mr Jackson?"

"Does your daughter still have the barn at Halsall?"

"Oh." Manchu threw his arms up in the air and shook them above his head. " She does. Yet she does nothing with it. It still be only a roof and three brick sides. She live in a caravan while they find the time to start on it. They live in that caravan until they have grandchildren this way they go. Why? You want to buy a barn? Talk some sense into them?"

"Not buy, but I might like to borrow it over the next few weeks. I'd only need it for a couple of hours each day. Do you think she'd oblige?"

"What do you want it for? Nothing illegal, Mr Jackson, I hope?"

Chris pretended to be affronted at the suggestion. "You'll probably laugh, but I want to learn to dance secretly, and my friend here is an excellent teacher. I have a bet on that I won't do well in a competition. I want to win that bet, so I don't want to be seen dancing before the event."

Manchu chuckled. "I give you her phone number. She will love the subterfuge." He turned to Gina. "Maybe in exchange you can teach them a dance to do at their wedding next year."

"Well, that went well. Easier than I expected," Chris said, after Manchu had gone through to the back. "It is still in the open air, but it has a roof, we can use lamps, and the surface is a properly flagged floor. I'll phone her later."

They started on their main course, but Chris put his knife and fork down mid-meal.

"I've been thinking about Valentine's Day. Can we skip going to the Wirral? Let's stay nearer home and fit a bit more into the day without all the travel. Time's a bit short if I have to be back for half-five or thereabouts. What about nipping into Southport instead?"

Her hopes of a lovely romantic day out, and the possibility of Chris stopping overnight, disappeared. Part of her had hoped he hadn't meant it when he said he couldn't stay out in the evening; that he really did have the time free and was making excuses because he wasn't into the whole Valentine's thing.

She forced herself to smile, and agreed to do something locally.

"Good. Glad you don't mind. Why don't we eat at the hotel they've done up on Lord Street? I believe it's changed drastically since it was taken over." He picked up his knife and fork and carried on eating.

Her appetite for the fillet steak waned. She found it was sticking in her throat as she tried to swallow. Chris finished his plateful and she was still less than halfway through hers.

She pushed the plate away. "I'm sorry, I can't eat anymore, I'm full."

"No worries." He called to Manchu for the bill. "I need to go into the station tonight, go over my report on the stuff we found, but if you like we could run through our foxtrot turns and shorter steps again for an hour, at yours, and I'll still be able to get there before Terry's shift ends."

They spent an hour practising the foxtrot. Her mind wasn't fully on the dance steps and she made simple errors which were out of character for her. As she sorted out the music system and changed the batteries in the remote control at the end of their practice, Chris stood behind her with his arms around her middle and his chin on her head.

"What's the matter, Gina? You don't seem yourself?" His arms slid from her waist to arrive gently at her shoulders, moving slightly so he was standing in front of her. He was between her and the music system, preventing her from finishing her tidying, so that she had to face him.

"What's wrong? Don't say 'nothing', because I know something's on your mind."

His touching and sympathetic search of her face as he asked the question was too much for her to take. She couldn't tell him that she thought he was lying about Valentine's evening, and she was wondering what he was trying to cover up.

"Nothing really." He raised his eyes to the ceiling, and she needed to think of something to satisfy him. After a few seconds, she shrugged. "I suppose I'm thinking of the events of the day. Do you really think that guy recognised me? I sometimes wonder why I've had such a run of bad luck this year, and I'm beginning to suspect he may have a grudge. Perhaps he knew I'd reported the vandalism to the police. Or maybe he finds me an easy, weak target, or something."

"That's your imagination running away with you, sweetheart." He stroked her cheek with the back of his fingers and kissed her forehead. "He's a chancer. It will be a coincidence. Who could hold a grudge against you? You're such a wonderful, loving and caring person. No one would want to hurt you deliberately."

Chapter Seventeen

The rain beat on the windows of the restaurant, large drops drumming out of time with the beat of her heart, making her almost dizzy. Chris had arrived holding a bunch of velvety, dark red roses. Not a dozen, possibly five or six, but as her house was still full of the flowers from his bouquet, it would have been a waste of money buying more. She'd apologised for her small gift to him, a bow tie in the same colour as the dress she planned to wear for the foxtrot competition.

Manchu's daughter, delighted at the thought of learning a special wedding dance, had allowed them the use of the barn, even turning up one afternoon to watch. They used their few days of being together to fine-tune the foxtrot routine, practising over and over from ten in the morning through to the fading light. Chris made a picnic each day to eat in the breaks, and she provided the music. He enthused about it being seamless and perfect, when she knew it still needed a few tweaks, but their dedication, even in the cold and damp February air, had certainly paid off.

He'd been the perfect Valentine throughout the day. Plenty of hugs and kisses, walking with arms around the other, sheltering close together in small doorways from the persistent rain. Now she sat opposite the man responsible for the pounding of her heart, the tingling in her bones and the fluttering in her stomach. If she had any more love overload symptoms she'd be in hospital, with the doctors and nurses bending over her saying, "She can't take anymore, her heart is going to explode, stand back!"

"I wish I was with you in your world."

His words, seemingly from the distance, broke into her thoughts.

"Um, pardon?"

"Where were you Gina? I've been talking to you and you're on some other planet. Are you ok?"

She looked at him, his tousled hair, tamer than usual because, as they'd entered the restaurant, he'd taken out his comb and combed the wet hair back into place. When they followed the front of house manager to their table, some of the strands had rebelled and flopped back. She wanted to reach out and touch them, and then touch his cheek and lips.

"Hello? Earth to Gina?"

"I'm having a lovely day."

"Are you? You seem miles away, instead of here with me." He wore his concerned look, the one where his beautiful blue eyes narrowed and his tanned forehead furrowed.

"Oh, I am with you, but in my thoughts it isn't raining, and we're warm and cosying up in bed. Despite the rain, this has been a perfect day so far."

"The roses were a bit of a damp squib though, weren't they? A cheesy cliché?"

"No! No, they were lovely, honestly."

He reached across the table and gently stroked her hand before holding it.

"I was going to buy you a spa day at the Dunesands, but I thought you'd rather have this instead." He used his other hand to burrow inside his jacket and pull out an envelope. "I hope you like it."

She took it from him and opened it. The picture on the front showed two kissing rabbits, with the words, *To The One I Love.*

"Aw, it's lovely. Cute." She fiddled with her napkin. A faint ripple of pleasure ran through her. "Do you? Love me, I mean."

"You know I do." He made a kissing motion. "Open it."

As she opened the card, a slip of paper fell onto the table. She picked it up and her jaw dropped. In her hand was a receipt for the final demand bill which he'd obviously paid for her.

She didn't know what to say. On the one hand, she was

grateful to him for helping her out. On the other she'd said no to his help, but he'd gone behind her back and must have taken the bill with him. No wonder she couldn't find it, and she'd searched through all her bins too.

He was watching her, his expression showing he was gauging her reaction. Even in her confused state, she knew she had to be careful not to over-react and spoil the day.

"Thank you. That was a nice thing to do, but I did say I didn't want you to pay it."

"I couldn't stand by and watch you struggle. I had the money. I could have splashed it out on something totally unnecessary, like beauty products or treatments, which you absolutely do not need, or I could've used it to take a weight off your mind. I chose the latter. You're not mad at me?"

He gave her a look with such big puppy-dog eyes that she had to smile.

"Can we call it a loan? I'll pay you back when I'm able. But it has helped, a lot, especially in the light of everything going on at the moment."

He took hold of her hand again. "If it makes you happy then I'll agree to that, for now. But if you do pay it back, it goes straight into paying for the Spa day I first thought of. Deal?"

She nodded reluctantly, and he pretended to shake her hand to seal the agreement, only to have to let go and sit back in his chair as the waitress approached with their food. She also sat back in her chair until the silver service waitress finished fussing over their plates and another waiter had served them vegetables from silver dishes.

"Do you own your own home?" she asked, once the waiter had left. "I seem to remember you saying that you pay for it each month, but you didn't say if it was mortgage or rent."

"I live in my parents' home. It's a long story, but to cut it short, Mum and Dad had a lovely home, a large detached, three-bedroomed Victorian home with a lot of sprawling garden. They bought a terrace in Southport to start their married life, and before I was born they mortgaged it start up Dad's business. He did very well, paid off his loans and bought the house I was eventually born in. I'm an only child, so Mum was able to help out in the office side of the business. Then Dad had a mini-stroke at work. Luckily the customer acted quickly and got him to hospital, but it took a long time for him to recover. He did, but the business was losing money, and trying to keep it all going was affecting his health. He wanted to close his business but his employees had a right to a pay-off, and he needed more money than he had in the business to do that. He sold the house and they rented a smaller one. The stroke stopped him dancing with Mum, he no longer had a business, no longer owned his own home, and he became a different man. He felt useless, a failure, wouldn't go out, became depressed and then suffered another stroke."

She listened to him without interruption, and when he paused, she searched her mind for something to say. She remembered her gran and grandad and the problems they'd had later on. All she could manage was, "Oh, Chris."

"He became too difficult for my mum to cope with on her own, so I moved back home. When Dad died, my mum carried on paying the rent and I chipped in my share. Now I've taken on the rent. That's why I said Tony was damn lucky to pay as little as he did, and why I understand how you are finding it difficult. There's no shame in admitting it, and I don't mind helping you pay your bills while you're looking for a job."

"Thanks, but no thanks, I don't want to be a kept woman." She wished she could retract the last bit when Chris drew back from her. She'd offended him and the atmosphere cooled a little. The day had gone so well until the moment she reacted over the paid bill. Now she had to try to put things right. "You could always move in with me and share the upkeep." There, she'd said it. She gave him what she hoped was a dewy-eyed look, something akin to the appealing eyes of Thumper or Bambi.

He relaxed and laughed. "Stop giving me the eyes. I'd love to take you up on the offer one day. What red-blooded man could say no to sharing the bed of the loveliest, sexiest woman in Freshby every night?"

She wrinkled her nose at him, but felt the heat rise in her cheeks. "I can feel a 'but' coming now."

"But – I have far too much furniture and paraphernalia to sort before I moved anywhere. I'd need at least six months' notice, possibly more. Sorry, not very romantic, I know. We will live together at some point in the future, though. I promise."

Like Cinderella, time ran out on her date. The conversation had flowed well, after the subject of Chris moving in had been dealt with, and neither of them realised how quickly the time was passing. They had to rush to the car park, making it with minutes to spare before the parking ticket ran out. Chris deposited her at the doorstep with a lingering kiss and the promise of longer, more intimate moments ahead, and then he was gone.

She looked at the clock: five forty-five. She'd already had a Prosecco with her meal at the restaurant, so she might as well open a bottle of wine and settle down to flick through the TV channels. She took the tousled-looking cuddly teddy and the Valentine card out of her handbag. Chris had bought her the teddy from a card shop sale, saying it had uncontrollable hair like his. The paws were embroidered with the words *Christmas Hugs*, and he said it would remind her of when they met. As if she needed reminding! The two cute bunnies on the card smiled up at her and she caught herself smiling back at them. *To The One I Love.* He'd certainly made her feel loved today. It was a shame he had to work tonight, but he *had* promised they would live together, and that was good enough for her to dream about. She placed her glass of wine on the coffee table and opened the card.

His handwriting was neat and he'd drawn little hearts all around the sides of the card, but it was the words that made her heart sing. She hadn't noticed them in the restaurant.

I love you so much. I'd give you the world if you asked.

Another sleepless night had Gina up at five-thirty, dressed, showered and out for a walk within the half-hour. Having bumped into Richard twice on her morning walks, she chose a different route to the dunes, and decided to walk through the pinewoods, to where she and Chris had danced in the car park.

The direct route from her house to the pinewoods took her past Chris's house. She could avoid his road completely and it would add five minutes to her walk, or she could do what she thought of after drinking half the bottle of wine last night. She could surprise him by knocking at his door, send him off to work with a kiss, and show him what he was missing in delaying moving in together.

When she came within sight of the top of his road, a quick check of the time told her it was almost six-thirty. It could go either way. If he was in a rush to get out to work, he might be annoyed at the delay, or possibly be so pleased to see her he didn't care if it made him late. She reached his road sign, made her decision, and picked up her pace to get to his house.

The butterflies were building in her stomach and her heart beat a little faster when she saw his car, but what she saw next caused her to falter, and left her feeling flat. Next to Chris's car was another, the same size but darker. Her mind went back to the night on the bus when she wasn't sure if she had missed spotting his house, or if there had been two cars in the drive. What should she do? The simplest explanation was that he already had a visitor. If he had a lodger, surely he would have told her by now?

She kept her head facing away from his house, thankful she'd worn her dark jacket and pull-on hat, and hurried past his gate. With a bit of luck nobody would see her. Deep in thought, she barely noticed the route she was taking until she reached the pinewoods. Maybe she should have knocked? If there was a simple explanation, she wouldn't be worrying now. She laughed at herself. Why hadn't she knocked at the door anyway, instead of scurrying off?

The aroma of the pinewoods, strongly scented first thing in the morning, revived her spirits, and buoyed by the reasoning that she would have discovered a simple explanation had she knocked, she continued along the paths.

Gina loved being outdoors first thing in the mornings. As well as the cheery 'Hellos' and 'Good mornings' from the dog-walkers, the birds were at their most vocal, and the red squirrels came out of hiding. The path took her down beyond the tall pines to the flat-topped trees, and eventually the squat trees petered out into the thick dune grasses. She breathed in the strong salty smell of the sea, before turning back, and walking past the car park area to the end of the pinewoods.

The cold fresh air and stimulating walk had cleared her head of all doubts she'd had about the other car in Chris's drive, so this time she had no qualms walking along his road on the way home. She wasn't prepared for what she saw as she approached his house.

His car wasn't in the drive, but it was after nine o'clock so she expected him to be at work. However the darker car, a navy-coloured one, was still there. As she slowed her pace to collect her thoughts, a young woman with blonde hair tied up in a ponytail opened the front door, went out to the car and took a large supermarket shopping bag out of the boot. A few groceries fell out of the bag when she placed it on the path to close the boot. As she gathered them up and picked up the bag to return back to the house, Gina, who by now was almost at his gate, got a clear view of her.

She was probably three, possibly five years younger than herself – and most definitely pregnant.

Chapter Eighteen

Gina wanted to run home. The ringing in her ears threatened to become deafening, and the loud pounding of her heart, in competition with it, was making her nauseous. All the way back to her house, her head ached with her thoughts chasing around and around and coming to no conclusion.

Once through the door, she ran upstairs, tossed the newly-acquired teddy aside and flung herself on the bed.

So, she thought, the reason he couldn't see me on Valentine's evening was because he had to be at home with his pregnant partner.

That would make sense. He had to be home early enough to get ready and go out. The dark-coloured car she'd spotted in the drive, the night she had to get the bus to and from work, was the one in his drive early this morning. The thought kept taunting her that he had never offered to stay overnight. He was always rushing off home at a reasonable hour. She even wondered if he'd really been in Manchester on a course for four days the previous week, or had he been at home with his partner?

No wonder he doesn't want to live with me, if he's already living with someone else.

She was tormented by her thoughts until, exhausted, she dozed off, only to be woken by her phone. It was still in her pocket, and by the time she realised it was actually her phone ringing and where the sound was coming from, it had stopped. She scrolled through her missed calls. It was Chris's number. The phone started again while it was in her hand. She made a decision, and pressed the decline key. She didn't want to talk to him. What could she say that described the way she felt? What could he say, if he didn't tell her the truth? She didn't want to hear any more lies.

The voicemail light flashed on the screen. Not wanting to hear his voice, she put her phone on the bedside table and walked to the wardrobe to choose some different clothes for her planned trip to the job centre.

She glanced at the phone a couple of times as she changed into her navy trousers and cream round-neck jumper. Chris never phoned her during his working hours, so why was he phoning her now? Had he seen her pass his house on her morning walk? Was he now feeling guilty? Or would he make some weak excuse? She made a mental note to ask Shelley to quiz Geoff later about Chris's relationships, and steeled herself for another day of job-hunting.

"How's it going? Sorry I've not been in touch, I've been rushed off my feet with Geoff still incapacitated." Shelley phoned her an hour or so after she arrived home. Gina was about to make herself a snack, since she'd missed lunch, and besides being hungry she was weary and low in spirits. "Any luck finding a job? Did you have a good day with Chris yesterday?"

Gina opened her mouth to tell Shelley about the job centre, but instead of words a large sob escaped, and then another, and another…

Shelley tried to pacify her.

"Gina. Whatever's wrong? I didn't mean to make you cry, love, I just thought I'd phone to catch up on the news. I presume the job-hunting hasn't gone well. I'd come round to yours, but I'm on my own here. I only phoned because there's been a bit of a lull. Please don't cry. If you come here, I can make us a brew and when Geoff gets back from the wholesalers he can take over while we go in the back for a chat." She wouldn't let Gina refuse. "I need to go. Customers! Get yourself over here and let your Aunty Shelley make you feel better. I'm expecting you!"

Gina huffed to herself in resignation. If she didn't go over to the shop, Shelley would hot-foot it over to her house when they closed, and her Argentine tango class would be there by then. She carried on making the snack, because if Shelley kept her talking she mightn't have time to eat before the class tonight either.

The cheese had just browned and she'd switched the grill off when there was a loud hammering at the door. She put the grill pan to one side, and went to answer the door wiping her hands on the tea towel as she walked. She dropped the tea towel in surprise as she came face to face with her visitor.

"Your bell doesn't work! I've had to knock twice too!"

Gina had to make a conscious effort to keep from making a sharp retort to Paula. The woman was dressed in a three-quarter-length, leopardskin faux fur coat over a straight leather skirt. Her dyed blonde hair was piled on her head in a perfect topknot, and she wore long false eyelashes and heavily-drawn eyes with black eyeliner reaching out from the outside corner of each eye by at least half an inch. Her right leg was encased in plaster up to the knee and she leant heavily on her crutches.

"If you move back a bit, I can come in. I don't intend to do my talking on the doorstep."

Still speechless, Gina stepped aside to let Paula hobble past. As she closed the door, she spotted Richard in his car outside her gate. He waved, and she waved back and smiled. Did he just give her a thumbs-up? How strange! She replied with a smaller wave and closed the door.

Paula was in the doorway of her dance room. Her top lip curled up as she took in the detail.

"It's very small! How do you manage to teach anything in here? The only things it has in its favour are the beautiful large mirrors."

"Have you just come to criticise and gloat, or do you have a valid reason for your visit? If you have more to say, do you want to sit down and take the weight off your leg?" She pointed ahead to the dining room and motioned for Paula to decide for herself.

Paula chose to sit on the chair in the dance room. She rifled through the music and dance notes on the table by the music centre.

"Good choice of music. I always think it best to use the

modern contemporary music for latin, rather than the old tired stuff."

"I'm glad it meets with your approval." Gina didn't try to hide the sarcasm in her tone. The day had already been too much to bear, without having to put up with Paula's sneers and snide comments. "But now, if you don't mind, can you cut to the reason for your visit? I'm sure you're not here to chat about the latest trends in pop music and home decor. What can I do for you?"

"It's more what *I* can do for *you*. I'll come straight to the point. You need a job. I need a teacher. Are you interested?"

Gina's eyes widened at the offer. Surely she'd misheard her. The last thing she'd expected was Paula offering her a job; she must be in a bad way with her leg. She stifled a laugh.

"I thought you'd come to offer to buy the mirrors!"

"You think I'm joking? I can't teach at the moment. I've tried, but it hasn't been successful. I don't know how long this will go on for." She pointed at her leg. "It could be weeks, or months. Either way I need someone to step in and teach. Full-time, living wage. I need an answer now."

Gina hesitated. She needed the job, and this was possibly an offer sent from the gods. On the other hand, it could be a slippery slope ending with a jump into hell. Could she work with Paula, and have her as a boss?

"When do I start?"

"Is that a yes? Starting tomorrow, and let's say a probationary period of eight weeks? We should know by then if we can work together. I will know more about the state of my leg too. If we survive each other's company for eight weeks, there will be a permanent job for you, although it may not be full-time. We'll have to see what happens."

Gina could tell that Paula was worried about her leg, and how fit she'd be to dance again. She softened slightly towards her. "That sounds fine to me... and thank you."

Paula gave her a brief nod in acknowledgement. "It was Uncle Richard's idea, but I accept it was one I hadn't thought of, and the best we could come up with."

Well, Gina thought, that was a backhanded compliment. I

bet she isn't used to giving them out. She'll probably be a hard taskmaster too. Aloud, she said, "So, tomorrow?"

"Ten-thirty tomorrow morning. I'll run through the way I work and the timetables. I realise you have your own class here. We will work around that for now." Paula eased herself up from the chair. "That's all. Don't be late, I don't like tardiness."

Gina opened the door and Paula hobbled passed. While she had her head down negotiating the step and pathway, Gina saw Richard raise his head from his newspaper, so she gave him the thumbs-up and mouthed *Thank You*.

Shelley nudged the door shut with her hip and placed the mugs of tea on the table in front of Gina.

"Geoff said he doesn't know anything about Chris's relationships. They don't really delve into things like that. If it crops up in conversation, they might chat, or ask the odd question, but it never has. He's always taken it that Chris was single because he didn't mention any women or talk about his home life. Anything he's joined in with, at the club or pub, he's always been on his own, even if some of the others took their other halves."

"Strange that no one really knows a lot about him. I presume the men in the police think he keeps himself to himself, or at least that's the impression Richard gave me. One of them at the ball made a comment that he'd 'kept me quiet' as though he is secretive, and he does seem to be anxious to keep to timings. Then there was the day we, well, you know…" Her cheeks burned and she knew she'd blushed because Shelley did her exaggerated winking face again. "Anyway, he sort of… interrupted the moment to make a phone call before following me upstairs. I didn't think it strange at the time, but knowing what I know now…"

"What do you know, Gina, eh? You saw a woman."

"A pregnant woman."

"Ok, you saw a pregnant woman go into his house. You've spotted her car outside a few times. So? It could be his sister. She could be hiding from an abusive boyfriend and doesn't want people to know where she is."

"He's an only child."

"Not sister then. What about a cousin? Could be a cousin, or an ex-girlfriend he stayed friends with and he's helping her out through a difficult time. Not ideal, I know, but it's a possibility." Shelley slurped her drink. "Or a lodger. Could be a lodger, but he's not told you in case you think there's more to it than there is."

"You think I'm making mountains from molehills?"

"I think you should ask him, Gina. Give him a chance to explain. He doesn't strike me as the sort of man to be a love rat. Now Tony for instance – for Tony, I'd have had the rat bait ready as soon as he stepped through the door. You can tell Chris loves you, Gina. Even Geoff has mentioned how besotted he is over you, and for Geoff to notice that it must be true. We came home from a weekend away and Geoff didn't notice the bungalow next door was missing – demolished! It had been gone for at least a month, and he only noticed because he had to take some post around and couldn't find the letterbox! I'm kidding about the letterbox, by the way. He discovered it when he couldn't find the door!"

Gina snorted her tea and Shelley passed her a tissue to wipe her chin and jumper.

"That's better, love. There'll be some sort of obvious explanation. My advice is to ask him. If he tells you the truth, and you don't like it, well, at least you'll know, won't you?"

"Shelley, the voice of reason." Gina raised her mug in a toast. "You've made your point, and yes, I suppose you're right. I'll ask him, and then I'll know for certain."

Chapter Nineteen

There was still time to phone Chris before the students turned up for their Argentine tango class. She'd promised Shelley she'd call him as soon as she got home. The phone stared at her from the kitchen table. There'd been three missed calls from Chris and a voicemail. She took a deep breath, clicked on voicemail and listened.

"Hi Gina. I called at yours this morning around seven, but you were probably still in bed. I wanted to see you before I left, but will try phoning you again later. I'm going to be away for a few days. Got the call late last night. One of the guys has dropped out and my name was next on the list, so a bit short notice. Speak soon. Love you."

She looked at her calls log. The last missed call was lunchtime. Where was he and why? She pressed call back. It was silent for a few seconds, and then she heard *It has not been possible to connect your call*. She put the phone back on the table. He was either out of signal range, or he had his phone switched off. She'd try later, after her class was over.

As it happened, the class didn't run smoothly. It seemed everyone had their problems. She was talking to Dorothy about an upset during her voluntary work at a local nursing home, when Darren burst into the room.

"Is Mercury in retrograde or something?" he asked of anyone listening. "Everything's gone wrong today. Everything!" He threw his hands out wide to demonstrate how much everything was. Basil was looking sulky, and merely grunted. Jonathon, who usually chatted to Darren, was quiet and withdrawn.

Gina put her own problems aside to concentrate on her students and the new steps she was teaching them.

"No, Darren. Step back with your right foot first. Your right foot! This part of the dance sequence is one you've done before." As she was trying to sort out Darren's steps, all she could hear in the background was Basil arguing with Jonathon. She saw Darren and Dorothy exchange knowing looks.

"Jonathon is far too patient, especially with *him*." Dorothy kept her voice low, but her nod towards Basil made it obvious she was talking about them. "He needs to stand up for himself. Basil is a bully, just like that volunteer I was telling you about, Gina."

At that moment Jonathon did stand up for himself. "You need to let me step around to the back. I have two steps to make before the gancho, and then it's your turn to move." He twisted around to look at Gina. "Tell him Gina, please. I'm sure he's doing it on purpose. He's almost taken chunks out of my shins from gancho-ing when he's not supposed to."

"Let me see what you're dancing," she said to them both. "Then I can see where it goes wrong."

"That's just it. I don't go wrong, it's him." Basil pointed accusingly at Jonathon. "He's useless. He can't do anything right. He can't dance the right steps, he won't go for promotion at work, he can't cook, he'll always be a skivvy, he's useless!" At the end of his outburst, he lashed out with his foot and caught Jonathon square on the knee, before storming out of the room and slamming the door as he left the house.

There was a stunned silence for a few moments. Darren was unusually lost for words. Jonathon bit his lip as he sat on the chair and rubbed his knee. Gina couldn't tell if he was trying not to cry, or suffering from the pain from the knee, or maybe both.

"Do you want some ice to put on it?" she asked.

"It'll be fine. My prides hurt more than my knee. I hate public displays like that. Sorry, guys, it's been a tough week, and it wasn't all about wrong dance steps tonight. This has been brewing for a while."

They were all surprised at what was, almost, a speech from Jonathon. They were even more surprised when he suggested going to the pub after class.

"So, mate," said Darren as he put the last of the drinks down in front of them all, "do you want to talk about it? If you don't, I'll happily start the ball rolling with my story of woe, from my working day."

Jonathon fiddled with his glass, turning and swirling the liquid in it, and sighed.

"The nursing care home where I work is closing. They are transferring the elderly residents to different homes in the area. It's been on the market for a long time, and the new owner is going to renovate and such like, then rebrand. No one will be able to live there while he's gutting it throughout. I was offered a desk job, running a care agency, which meant more money, and decent hours, and Basil is annoyed that I turned it down."

"Why turn it down? Was Basil tetchy because of the money side of things, or did he want you to have quality time with hours that fitted in with his? " Darren's voice became softer than usual with a compassionate tone. Gina realised that the brash, loud Darren everyone knew also had a caring side to him. She even wondered if he put on a loud front to disguise some vulnerability.

"Neither. He hates that my job is hands-on. Literally hates me being a manual worker, serving food, giving baths, cleaning up their toilet, not the sort of thing he feels able to talk about with his peers. He doesn't tell them what I do. He skirts around the subject, and once he even hinted I was a doctor! But I love my job. I'd rather be caring for the elderly than sitting behind a desk in an office. Basil doesn't understand that. He's been sulking since I told him I wasn't applying, and I burnt the tea when we had an almighty row about it, so that was the last straw to him. He loves his food."

"Aw, sorry mate, but you're right to stick to what you feel is best. At the end of the day, it is what you love doing and it brings home a wage. It's not as if you're doing it voluntarily like Dorothy, so he can't complain." Darren took a mouthful of his lager shandy and waited for Jonathon to carry on talking. When he didn't, Darren chipped in with his own grumble. "There's you turning down a job with more money, and me being turned down after my interview for a small promotion. It's the planets, I tell you. They're all over the place. What are you going to do?"

"I'll look for another care home. I have a month's notice, but if I find one sooner, they will let me go. I'll find a job, even if it's a bit further from home. Trouble is, I'm not sure Basil will compromise. He's been so bad-tempered and stroppy over the whole job thing, and he got really nasty towards me a couple of nights ago. That's why I thought he was gancho-ing into my leg deliberately during the dancing. Was your interview today, Darren?"

Darren ran with his tale of woe, as he called it. Jonathon sat back to listen, and Gina smiled to herself. Jonathon hardly spoke at class, hiding in the shadow of Basil who always had something to say, most of which wasn't complimentary. After the surprisingly long conversation and opening up to their group, Jonathon deftly turned the conversation back to Darren, and let Darren do what he did best: talk.

Gina listened to his re-enactment of the interview, word for word, complete with actions. Darren could tell an entertaining dramatic tale, and she sympathised and tutted in all the right places. What she wasn't prepared for was the genuine catch in his throat, when he owned up that he'd made a mistake to his original boss, who then told him he'd hoped to get rid of him from the department.

"Surely he didn't actually mean that. Had he badly phrased it?" she asked.

"No, unfortunately, I made a huge error, listing a car for sale at two thousand pounds instead of twenty-thousand pounds. The guy was inundated with phone calls and wasted viewers, and rang the sales department to complain. So when I came out of the interview, the boss was livid. To quote his exact words: 'I'd hoped to offload you onto their unsuspecting department, but now I know they're not happy with you, and we're not happy with you, and the customer isn't happy with you, I don't want you on my team much longer. You are on a warning. Another mess-up like that and you are out.' So, that's my sorry tale, and now I need to find another job as well."

"Can't you apply for that administration job Jonathon didn't want to apply for? Or is it too late, Jonathon?" said Dorothy.

While the two men discussed the details of the job, Dorothy moved nearer to Gina and said quietly, "Is everything alright? You seem subdued. Is it the intruder business that's worrying you?"

"I haven't heard anything more from the police about that yet. I imagine they are still busy investigating it though. I'll be fine, Dorothy. I just have a few relationship problems I need to work through."

"I thought everything was progressing nicely with you and that nice young policeman." Then Dorothy laughed, "I know all policemen look young these days, once you pass a certain age." She placed her hand on top of Gina's. "Do you want to talk about it?"

"Not much to say really, until I can talk to him to get the facts and some real answers. He's away for a while and either hasn't got a signal on his phone, or isn't answering it."

"Well, you know where I am if you need a shoulder." Dorothy gently rubbed Gina's back with her free hand, before turning to the two men, who'd finished talking about jobs and moved onto films. "Darren, love, you *are* still able to drive after that shandy, aren't you? Could I trouble you for a lift home?"

Left on their own, Jonathon turned to Gina and asked if he could stay over at hers for the night. "Just to let Basil cool down and allow me to sort things out in my own head, you understand. I don't want to stay longer than a night, but I don't want to crawl back in tonight or he will take it as me being weak. He likes to be in control, you see."

"That's fine with me. To be honest with you, it will be good to walk back home with someone, even if Mrs Renwick thinks I'm the neighbourhood slapper." She laughed when she saw the puzzled expression on Jonathon's face. "I'll explain later. Don't be disappointed when you see the meagre offerings in my fridge and cupboards, but I think I have enough to rustle up a breakfast for you."

"Thanks, you're an angel. If you're not in a hurry, I'll have a wine. Shall I get one for you too, or would you prefer something stronger?"

She agreed to a wine, and as Jonathon went to the bar, she wondered what had made her say she'd be glad of the company. She didn't want company, she wanted to be left alone to sort out her own thoughts. The day wasn't yet over, but so much had happened, she wasn't sure which was the more appropriate response to events. Should she laugh or cry? She was obviously thankful to have a job, especially after hearing Jonathon and Darren discuss their problems, but the prospect of working with Paula was daunting, and the person she wanted to talk it over with was living with someone else.

The rain had stopped by the time they left the pub. Darren had given everyone a lift to the Freshby Arms, rather than the one nearest to Gina's house, so they stood in the doorway and discussed getting a taxi back, before deciding to walk.

The journey home took her past Chris's house. Knowing he was allegedly away for a few days, she braced herself for what she might find in his driveway.

On the way, she found herself telling Jonathon about Chris. She hadn't meant to, but he had offloaded all his doubts about his relationship with Basil, not for her to solve, just for him to release his thoughts and un-jumble them in the telling. Her response to him had been similar. She was relaxed in his company, he was a good listener, and the drink had loosened her tongue. So as they approached Chris's house, it seemed natural to her to point it out to Jonathon.

"See, there's a car in the drive and it isn't Chris's. It's the other car I was telling you about. Why is it there at this time of night? Why?" She wasn't actually asking a question, even though she wanted to know. Her chest had begun to tighten and she felt physically sick. The wine probably hadn't helped her stomach cope with the upset either. She inhaled slowly and deeply, and breathed out slowly through her mouth.

Jonathon remained silent. He linked her arm and supported her as they walked past the drive. It was only as they drew close to Gina's road that he spoke.

"There's something about that car in his drive that seems

familiar. I've been wracking my brains trying to think what it is, but nothing is coming. I think I recognise the collection of teddies on the back shelf. If it springs to mind, I'll let you know."

"Remember I said I'd tell you why my neighbour will think I'm a loose woman, bringing you home. Look!" She put her key in the door, and turned to wave at Mrs Renwick who was, as usual, standing at her window. "She's watching me. I swear she only lives to spy on me."

"Gina, I can't tell if she's waving or beckoning to us."

Gina looked. "You're right, she really looks as though she *is* beckoning. That's strange, she doesn't usually. Do me a favour, Jonathon. Could you nip across and see what she wants, and I'll put the kettle on. She's probably being nosey and wants to know your name and your whole family history."

Jonathon dutifully went to see what Mrs Renwick wanted, so Gina left the door unlocked for him to enter, slipped off her coat and, after slinging it over the bannister, went through to the kitchen.

In the doorway, she froze.

Chapter Twenty

The floor by the sink was a mess of broken glass, milk, tomato sauce, and by the look of it, mud. The room smelt of dog muck, which made her wonder if the red liquid was maybe blood not tomato sauce, especially as both were on the sink, and the kitchen base, and... Her heart sank as she looked at the broken window.

She heard a sound coming from the corner wall, by the door to the garden, and breathed a sigh of relief. They must have gone, whoever it was. Her first thought was to clean up, when she remembered that she'd have to report it to the police. Her mobile phone was in her handbag, which she'd slung on one of the sofas in the dining room. She moved slightly to change direction and felt grit and crunching under her shoe.

"Ugh." She couldn't help speaking out loud. She was sure there'd be glass everywhere, so on top of everything else, she would have to face a day of cleaning the kitchen. Groaning inwardly, she kept her gaze on the floor to avoid more shards of glass as she carefully made her way to the dining room.

A forearm across the front of her neck knocked the breath out of her, and the almost choking hold caused her to lean backwards into her attacker behind her. She tried to breathe through her nose instead of her mouth, all the while struggling to free herself. The mix of body odour, drugs and other disgusting smells was overpowering, and her battle to keep from passing out became even more urgent, when she realised that he was trying to manouvre her towards the knife-holder near the oven.

She caught a movement out of the corner of her eye, just as her attacker kneed her in the back, making her legs buckle under her...

Jonathon was bending over her. His mouth was opening and closing but there was more than one voice, and she couldn't make his lips fit the words. She scrunched her eyes shut, waited for a few seconds then opened them again, in the hope of lipreading and making sense of everything.

Two voices and two faces leaned over her. She could see up their nostrils and she somehow found that amusing, so amusing that she started to giggle. The sound came from her stomach and rumbled its way through to her throat and out of her mouth before she could stop it. A weird mix of nerves and hysteria, high-pitched and trembling.

Jonathon stooped lower until he was almost face to face with her. She could see the concern in his eyes, and as if he had triggered a switch, her giggles bubbled over into racking sobs, so violent she couldn't catch a breath, and her heaving chest retched over and over.

"Gina! Gina, it's okay. You're okay. They've taken him away." Jonathon spoke softly, his voice soothing and hypnotic. "Breathe slowly. That's it, in and out, in and out."

She followed his guidance, all the while thinking that it was no wonder he wanted to remain working as a carer; he was a natural. He made her feel safe, his voice reassuring, repeating everything calmly. He was right and Basil was wrong. What if she was wrong? She wanted Chris to be here. Chris should be kneeling on the floor talking to her, putting his arms around her and telling her everything was going to be alright. But Chris wasn't here, and Jonathon was the one reaching out to lift her up off the floor. Mike Holmes was the one helping Jonathon to steady her and guide her to a chair, and Jonathon would be the one sleeping in her house overnight. Why couldn't it be Chris sleeping here tonight, in her bed, with his arms wrapped around her and his voice soothing and reassuring? Her lip quivered and her tears escaped and ran slowly down her cheeks.

"Sorry." What was she sorry for? Sorry that she was crying? Sorry that she wished they were someone else, or sorry that she had unwittingly dragged Jonathon into her mess?

"You've had a shock. That was a natural reaction, and

shouldn't happen again now."

"Thanks, Jonathon." She coughed, her voice sounded husky and her throat was sore. "You are still staying overnight, aren't you?"

"Of course."

"You're staying overnight? I thought Chris…" Mike had the grace to stop mid-sentence. Gina groaned, but Jonathon spoke for her.

"I've had a tiff with my boyfriend, so Gina kindly let me stay here for the night."

Mike nodded. "Well when the team have finished you can tidy up. There is someone on the way to board up the window. I just need to get the facts from you both, and then I'll leave." He turned to Gina. "Are you sure you don't want to go to the hospital to be checked over?"

She nodded her head, but wished she hadn't as her neck was still sore.

"If it gets worse I'll go along to A&E or the Walk-In Centre."

Mike opened his mouth to speak, paused for a moment, then took out his notebook.

By the time they closed the door behind Mike and the fingerprint team, Gina was too tired to tackle the mess. Jonathon had made them both a hot chocolate with the pods in her drinks machine, and then told her to get to bed and sleep off the feelings of shock. Before she got into bed, she rescued the teddy Chris had bought her and lay with her face in its soft fur.

When she awoke, it seemed as though she'd only slept for a few minutes. She had a sore throat when she swallowed, and a dull headache. It was an effort to get out of bed, but she managed it one leg at a time and slowly wrapped her dressing gown around herself. The man who'd boarded her window up the night before was calling back at ten to glaze it. She looked at the bedside clock. It was just after seven o'clock, which gave her three hours to clear the kitchen and buy some milk and bread for breakfast.

As she walked on to the landing, she saw the door to the bedroom Jonathon had used was open. She had a sneak look in; he'd made his bed and put the patchwork cover her gran had made neatly over the back of the squat boudoir chair. Maybe he'd already gone to work.

There was no sign of him downstairs either, but it was a pleasant surprise to discover that he'd cleared up the mess in the kitchen. A faint smell of lemon bleach, with undertones of floral air freshener, reached her nostrils. He'd made a thorough job of the cleaning, and when she looked in the bin to see what he'd used to clean it up, realised he'd even taken the bin bag outside and replaced it with a new one.

She was toying with the idea of making another hot chocolate for breakfast, when the sound of her front door being unlocked stopped her. Jonathon appeared in the doorway with a shopping bag. He'd been to Shelley's and bought bacon, egg, bread, milk and tomato sauce. He'd even bought items to replace the cleaning fluids he'd used, and bought a bunch of flowers for Mrs Renwick.

"You didn't have to do all the cleaning-up, but thank you, it's saved me a horrible job. If you tell me how much I owe you—"

"No need. I like a cooked breakfast, so I bought enough for two. I'll make it, you can make the pot of tea." He started sorting the bacon slices on to the grill plate. "How are you this morning? I can tell your throat is sore, your voice is husky." He continued to sort the eggs and bread without looking up. "I didn't replace the bottle of wine that got broken. Shelley said to tell you, if you call in this evening, she'll treat you to the wine, and you can drink it while you tell her the whole gruesome details."

Trust Shelley to know she'd need an ear to bend later. When Jonathon's cheeks began to redden, she wondered if he'd felt embarrassed letting her know he'd been talking to Shelley about her.

She managed to talk Jonathan into letting her pay for the flowers. After all, she reasoned with him, things could have been so much worse for her if it hadn't been for Mrs

Renwick's eagle eyes. She felt guilty for always thinking of her as a nosy busybody.

"That's great. I'll call in on Mrs Renwick on my way to Shelley's and give her the flowers to thank her, and have a neighbourly chat while I'm there. Shelley will help me relax, and I know now I don't have to worry about coming home on my own, because hopefully he is still under lock and key, or police watch, or whatever they do with suspects. Do you want to stay another night? I promise I won't expect you to clean any more rooms!"

"No thanks, Gina, but thank you for allowing me to stay here, I think I have it all sorted in my head now. I know what I should do." He carried on making the breakfast, and she didn't pry into his decision.

After he left for work she had a bath, dressed for her first day working for Paula, and dialled Chris's phone number again, knowing that the first thing Shelley would ask her was if she'd tried to contact him. It went straight through to the same automatic message as before.

Paula was already in the studio waiting for her, when Gina arrived at her dance school twenty minutes early.

"You're early, good! I don't waste time with small talk. You're here, so we may as well start work now."

Gina's mind was whirling like a carousel by lunch time. Paula had hardly paused for breath. She swapped from one subject to another without warning, threw in the odd test and question on things she'd told her an hour previously, and tapped her crutch on the floorboards if Gina's answer wasn't quick enough. Just when Gina thought she deserved a lunch break, Paula put the music on.

"I won't waste time with a break for lunch. You've clearly grasped the admin and rota side of things. Now I am going to play a compilation of songs from ballroom, latin and old time. What I want you to do now is to dance the steps appropriate for the beat and rhythm of that song. There will be no gap between them, so you'll need to think quickly. To make it more difficult, there will be several repetitions of beat. Do you understand me so far?" Gina nodded. "Good. The difficult bit is, for example, if you hear a waltz played for a second time, you change to dance the man's steps, for a third time, the woman's." Paula sat with a notebook, nodded for Gina to begin, and turned the speakers up.

When the music finally stopped, Gina looked at the clock on the wall behind Paula. She was tired, her neck ached, her head throbbed and her throat was so dry that every swallow felt like a box of needles passing through.

"You're good, but I expected nothing less." Paula looked at her notepad. "A slight hesitation between the cha cha and the fourth waltz, but otherwise a perfect score. You've done enough for today. Start the classes tomorrow with the Tinies at three o'clock." She was still looking at her notepad as Gina picked up her bag to leave. Was she expected to reply, or thank her?

"Bye. See you tomorrow, then."

Still Paula didn't look up. As Gina opened the door to leave, Paula said, "I love my uncle, and trust his judgement, but if I hadn't thought you good enough to keep up the excellent reputation of my school, I wouldn't have offered you the job. Not even as a temporary solution. Having put you through your paces today, I can see that if you'd had the money, and the premises, you could have had a school as successful as mine. Don't be late tomorrow."

"She said that? Blooming heck, Gina, that was praise indeed. You rock, girl!" Shelley put her hand up to high-five Gina. "The wine has been in the fridge since Jonathon told me about the ructions last night. Have you heard anything more from the police?"

"On the way home from Paula's, Mike Holmes – the policeman I told you about – was driving past and stopped. He said he'd tried a few times and couldn't get hold of me at home or on my phone. I'd had it switched off all day as I didn't want it ringing and annoying Paula. I got in the patrol car – goodness knows what everyone thought of that – and apparently the guy broke into mine while he was muddled with the drugs, thinking it was someone else's house. You'll never guess whose!"

"Tony's? Paula's? No, you'll have to tell me."

"Lucy's!"

"What!" Shelley spat out her mouthful of wine in shock. She grabbed a tissue out of the box and wiped down her top and the coffee table. "Sorry, good job it's white wine. Go on then, why Lucy?"

"Apparently he wanted more money from her, for jobs he'd done."

"What jobs?"

"Don't know. Mike didn't say. He just asked me which of my friends was a slim, fit-looking bird, bit of a toff with blonde hair, and tarted up all the time."

Shelley snorted again.

"You crack me up, Gina. I'm going to have to stop drinking while you tell the tale. It's a shame to waste this excellent wine."

"Mike made me laugh too. Apparently he quoted word for word what the guy said, when questioned at the station, in the hope I'd recognise the description of the woman he did the jobs for. I'm ashamed to say, that I did. What sort of friend does that make me?"

"Ex-friend, and rightly so." Shelley silently mouthed 'bitch'.

"Mike asked if I had a photo of her and where she lived. So I showed him a few pics on my phone and he made a copy of them and the contact details, and then said they'd be in touch."

"So it's still a mystery then? You know – what he did for Lucy."

"I've been thinking about it since. No doubt Lucy would have the use of Tony's car like I did, so that would solve the mystery of the car. But like you, Shelley, I can't figure out what sort of jobs she'd ask for and why."

Shelley made one of her exaggerated winks and tapped the side of her nose. Gina laughed out loud, and winced when her throat hurt.

"Sorry, I forgot about your throat. But you know, it takes all sorts with fetishes and such like."

"I hardly think that's the reason, well, not with Lucy anyway. Can you imagine?" She laughed with Shelley, and then they turned their attention away from Lucy, to spend a relaxed couple of hours discussing Paula, Geoff and the group from the Argentine tango class. She noticed that Shelley didn't mention Chris again after her immediate question about him, when Gina had first turned up at the shop, and she was glad to keep away from talking about him. Shelley was the tonic she needed to de-stress. She would deal with Chris face-to-face if she couldn't get hold of him on the phone before he came home.

Chapter Twenty-One

Paula was a hard taskmaster, and Gina had to grit her teeth and say nothing several times while teaching her Tinies class, as Paula butted in and corrected her over the smallest of details. She was nervous enough teaching the first few classes under Paula's beady and unforgiving eyes, but the text she'd had from Chis that morning had unsettled her, and she'd felt edgy and close to tears all day.

The last few adult classes had been much easier to teach. Paula left with strict orders to double-check everywhere was locked and lights off before Gina went home. It was said in front of the intermediate adult class, and when a few minutes had elapsed after Paula leaving, one of the men had announced "And – relax!" The class had joined in with the laughter.

Gina relaxed too, but said to them, "How do you know I'm not worse?" to which they'd all laughed even more.

"Impossible!" said the man.

She found herself enjoying the last few hours of teaching, but had been paranoid about leaving everything in the right place, turning out the lights and locking up. No doubt the more she did it, the less she'd worry. At home she changed into her pyjamas, made a hot chocolate and opened Chris's text again.

Are you ok? Tried to phone, will phone later. Text me, I'm getting worried. Can't wait to see you. Love you lots. C xxxxx

There'd been two missed calls from him that morning, one at five-thirty, the other at six. She'd been in a deep sleep making up for her lack of it the night before, combined with all the wine Shelley had administered to her in the name of therapy.

She'd slept until the clattering of the refuse lorries woke her up at eight. What was he playing at? Phoning her so early in the morning, but then his phone not being answered and apparently unavailable all day, it didn't make sense. What if she did text him? If there really was no signal, he wouldn't get the message anyway.

She thought about the pregnant woman she'd seen at his house. Maybe he was one of those men who strayed when their partner was pregnant and their sex life changed. It was a fact she'd read in women's magazines and the problem pages, that some men didn't find pregnant women attractive. Or if she was giving him some benefit of the doubt, maybe they'd only been going out a short time and the baby wasn't planned and he was just doing the right thing by standing by her. He certainly seemed caring enough for that to be a possibility, or maybe he realised he was trapped in a loveless relationship. She pressed *Call Back* on one of his missed calls, but got the same voice saying they couldn't connect the call. She checked the time – it was past midnight – no point trying to phone him again now. She slung the phone across the sofa, and went to bed.

She was being chased by Paula, and the smelly druggy guy, and she was chasing Lucy. Lucy found an old garage and managed to get through the door and lock it before she could reach her. The others were closing in on her. They were followed by the dropouts from the woods. She would forgive Lucy if she'd let her in the garage. She hammered on the door – "Lucy let me in! Let me in!" – "Go away!" – She thumped on the door again – and thumped and rang the doorbell, again and again... The others were almost upon her.

She sat bolt upright in bed. There was someone knocking at the door, and yes, that was her doorbell ringing. It was pitch black outside and a quick check of the clock told her she'd only been asleep for two hours. She put the light on to go down the stairs and let the person knocking know she was on her way. The knocking stopped.

"What the—? It's the early hours of the morning, what are you doing here?"

"Well, that's a lovely welcome, Sleepy Head!" Chris smiled at her. "I've driven all the way from the Outward Bound

Course in Scotland to spend a couple of hours snuggled up with you in bed, and you growl at me." He stepped past her into the hall. "We kept missing each other on the phone, and I was worried about you. I thought I'd drive down while the camp was asleep to see if everything was okay. Maybe check you over just to make sure." He gave her an impish grin that tugged at her heart, but she ignored it, instead giving into the anger boiling up inside her.

"Don't think you can play out your sexual fantasies with me! I'm not someone to be picked up when you're bored and things aren't going right at home, and then thrown aside as soon as everything is all hunky dory again."

Chris stepped back as though he'd been hit. His smile disappeared, his eyes narrowed.

"What the hell are you talking about? What sexual fantasies? I've passed up on a good night's sleep to drive all the way just to see you, and I know it's the early hours, but I thought you'd be as pleased to see me as I am to see you!"

"I can't believe you've turned up at this time. Is she asleep? Have you been home to her first and then sneaked out to see me, without disturbing her?"

"Is who asleep? Disturbing who? What are you talking about?"

He was certainly a good actor, although, she thought, the ability to remain deadpan probably came with his job.

"Your partner. The woman you live with. Don't deny it. I've seen her car outside at night as well as during the day. I've seen her, Chris, not just seen her, but noticed how pregnant she is."

At first he looked relieved as the penny dropped, but she watched as his expression quickly changed. His eyes darkened and his face reddened. She assumed the colour in his cheeks was embarrassment at being caught out.

"Did you think I wouldn't find out? Did you think because I was so lonely after chucking Tony out that I'd jump at the chance of a fling?"

She realised she'd made a mistake about the colour in his cheeks as soon as his voice lowered, and as if he was trying to keep some control over his words, he spoke to her slowly and deliberately.

"I can't believe you think so little of me, that you'd believe I'd cheat on a partner, and one you thought was a possibly pregnant partner at that! You don't know me at all, do you? I thought we had something special. I've just driven all the way from Scotland after an exhausting day, to be with you. For God's sake, Gina, who does that for a casual fling?"

That *she* might have been mistaken was starting to dawn on her. Her anger dissipated and she calmed down enough to defend herself.

"I didn't know you were in Scotland. In your voicemail you just said you were away! You could have been away with your partner, because there were no lights on in your house, and the other car parked in the drive all the time. What else am I to think? You could have kept your phone off, so I didn't phone while she was around. You could have nipped home early on Valentine's evening to take her out, or pack to go away the next day, I don't know. Maybe you're right, maybe I don't know you well. I thought I did, but I don't know why you won't stay overnight with me, I don't know why you rush back home or can't move in with me for months, or years, or whenever, if at all. You could be stringing me along."

Her list of things she didn't know were obviously not going to be answered, because Chris turned away from her, and without a word, left the house, walked down the path, got into his car and drove off.

Chapter Twenty-Two

Jonathon turned up to her dance class on his own. After he'd left her to go to work, the morning after the last class, he'd phoned in the evening to check she was still okay, and that was the last time she'd heard from him. He was a few minutes late and apologetic.

Relieved that he'd still turned up to dance, she asked him if things had settled down since she the last time they spoke.

"I've been looking for digs. Basil and I finally split for good last week. I've been staying in a B&B since he threw me out, but it's draining the small bit of savings I have. I'm going to need a deposit for a flat, so I can't keep paying holiday rates at boarding houses." He looked tired and pale.

"Anyway, I'm here now, and you don't want to hear my problems."

She wondered about offering him the spare room in her house for free, while he was looking for a place of his own. She hadn't heard from Chris since their argument five days ago, and doubted she would now, so it wouldn't make any difference to her love life having another person around. She took his hand and led him to the spot next to Darren and Dorothy.

"We'll have a cup of tea or coffee after class and see how we can help you." She counted out the beats to the music. "Ok, on the third beat one, two, three…"

They danced through the basic routine from start to finish. She was so pleased with the way the three of them had retained the steps, and their bodies had also become less stiff. She had them face the mirrors and walk with fluid movements towards them. They were used to her asking them to do this, as it made them aware of how slight changes in the way they moved could be sensual or comic. Obviously they were aiming for the suggestive, without being 'slutty' as Jonathon called it.

Darren, for all his cheeky antics and theatrical showiness, was very sensitive in his handling of, and actions towards, Dorothy. Dorothy on the other hand, could often be heard to say, "Come on Darren, I can do that. I'm not a porcelain doll!"

They were only two months into the class, and Darren and Dorothy were showing signs of being good enough to start taking their medal exams in the summer. Jonathon was growing in confidence since Basil had stopped attending the class, but now she needed to find him a partner. She didn't mind dancing with him, but it made it difficult to keep an eye on the progress of her students.

She took the remote control out of her pocket and switched to another, slightly quicker piece of music.

"Right, remember the new steps I taught you last week? Well, this time, I want you to dance through your basic steps, add two ganchos and an ocho, then follow that with the half giro, which if you remember is also called the media luna. The music is a bit quicker now so you have less time to think."

Darren and Dorothy went straight into their steps. Jonathon waited for her to take hold of him. They were just nearing the part of the routine for the gancho, when she thought she heard her front door open and steps in the hall. Wondering if it was Basil, she glanced at the door.

Chris looked into the room and raised his eyebrows as if asking for permission to enter. She made a face at him, which she hoped conveyed that he would have to wait. Her heart beat faster. Unsure of the reason for him turning up, she was confused as to how to play it: whether to be cool or friendly.

A noise in the hall, and Chris turning to see to it, changed her mind. Curious to see who he was talking to, she excused herself from Jonathon and made for the door.

"Here's someone you ought to meet." Chris didn't smile, but stepped aside to reveal a woman in her mid-sixties. She was a couple of inches taller than Gina's five foot two inches, and was very much the classic 'pear' shape; she was slim around the shoulders and bust, and widening out considerably from her ribs out over her very rounded stomach to her bottom. Her collar-length hair was thick, and curled, and the same brown as Chris's hair but with highlights of grey sprinkled through it.

"Oh, Christopher, they're dancing in here. It's lovely."

The woman rushed past Chris and into the middle of the room where she promptly started to do a solo waltz to the music. For a lady carrying a lot of weight around the middle she was extremely light on her feet. Darren and Dorothy stopped to look at Chris, then at the woman, then back at Chris waiting for an introduction.

With all eyes on him, Chris announced: "She's my Mum. She's called Kathleen." He held Gina's arm in a tight grip. "I need to talk to you." His crisp and business-like tone lacked the warmth she was used to.

"We're fine, Gina." Dorothy called. "You have your chat and we'll carry on here."

She waited until the class had turned away from them to entertain Kathleen, and turned to Chris.

"I don't understand what's going on here. I'm in the middle of teaching, Chris. Couldn't it wait until the end of class?"

"No, you wouldn't understand, because you didn't let me explain last week."

Behind her, laughter filled the room, but Chris had never looked so serious. She realised that whatever it was he had come to say was important to him, and she had the feeling it would impact on her too. He seemed to be mainly focused on the goings-on in the room behind her, rather than concentrating on talking to her.

"Do you want to sit in the dining room?"

"No, I'm better staying here in case I'm needed." He nodded towards the room, where there still appeared to be great hilarity. "If I'd waited until the end of your class it may have been a different Mum I brought. At the moment she is at her most lucid. It could all change hour by hour. I can't leave her on her own, and I needed to talk to you."

She nodded, all the while keeping her eyes on him, although he didn't look away from his mum and the group in the room.

"I thought you'd lost both your parents, the way you talked about them; as if they were in your past."

"I'm not here to have a long conversation. I agree, there are questions to be answered, but I don't have the time now. I need to know about the competition at the weekend."

"You mean you still intend to enter it with me?"

"We've put a lot of time and energy into getting it right. We can be professional about it, I'm sure. After all, many couples in competition are only partners in dance, not in life."

She swallowed down the lump which was developing in her throat. When she first saw him appear in the doorway, hope had sparked in her heart, but he'd managed to extinguish it with the end of his sentence. Well, she *was* a professional. If he still wanted them to enter the competition, she wouldn't argue.

Chants of "One, two, three, one, two, three," came from the studio. Dorothy peered around the edge of the door, and beckoned to them.

"You need to see this, it's wonderful."

They watched together from the doorway, Jonathon was guiding Chris's mum in a waltz around the room while Darren chanted the beat.

"Jonathon showed your mum a few steps from Argentine tango, Chris, and now she is teaching him the waltz."

The music stopped and Kathleen spotted Chris watching her.

"Christopher, watch carefully." She poked Jonathon in the chest. Gina noticed Chris frown. "Let's show my son what we can do. See if he can follow the steps too."

Darren turned the music back to the Argentine tango and Jonathon guided Kathleen through the basic steps. He didn't flinch when she caught him on the leg several times attempting the ganchos. Partway through she suddenly stopped, looked at Chris and announced she was tired and wanted to go home.

"When Mum says she wants to go home, she means immediately, Gina. I'll have to go. I'll pick you up at nine o'clock on Saturday morning. That should give us enough time to get to Southport and register."

"I can come back again, can't I?" Kathleen said.

Dorothy became the spokesperson for the class.

"Of course you can, Kathleen. We'd love to dance with you. You could dance with Jonathon again."

Kathleen clapped her hands as if applauding the class, then looking puzzled she stopped and turned to Chris.

"Take me home now!"

Gina watched as Kathleen linked her arm into Chris's and they left the house without a backward glance.

Gina put the kettle on for drinks, and got the cakes out of the cupboard. The others eased into the sofas in her dining room.

"Well, that was an eventful evening." Darren as usual started the conversation. "What a lovely lady Chris's mum is, I presume she isn't well. Has she got dementia or something?"

Gina had to admit that she didn't know, and it led to a discussion about Kathleen for a few minutes, before Gina, feeling uncomfortable about her lack of knowledge and details, changed the subject.

"Jonathon, I was very impressed with your waltz. Did you just pick that up tonight, or could you already do it?"

Jonathon blushed, and smiled as he answered. "I tried to teach myself to dance from *YouTube*. It's hard to follow when you need to face the opposite direction to the computer screen to do the steps. In fact, you can't follow it at all. Then, of course, you can't move much in a room the size of a shoebox anyway. I'd love to learn more dances. Maybe when your school grows in size you can add more classes."

She couldn't help thinking that Jonathon must have enjoyed his evening. He appeared more relaxed and willing to join in with the conversation, and was quite the star the way he danced with Kathleen. As she looked around the room, she could see how they were all relaxed and at ease with each other, and thanked chance that she had been sent such an amicable group of pupils.

"I can't see that happening for a long time, Jonathon, but I am hoping we can sort out your problem of somewhere to live. Are you booked in a room for tonight, or did you mean you needed somewhere to stay right away?"

"I could find a room easily in the cheap hotels, but I really want to have a permanent place to stay. I am booking rooms day by day at the moment. It isn't ideal."

She was about to make her suggestion, when Darren beat her to it.

"Sorted, mate," he said. "Come back to mine. I have a spare room. You can either stay permanently and pay towards my rent, or use it as a temporary base to search from. Either way, you're welcome to stay from tonight if you want to save the cost of a room. I owe you anyway. I went for an interview at that care agency you told me about, and they offered me the admin job. I start next week."

They all congratulated Darren, and as she watched Jonathon, she could tell he was touched by Darren's generosity. Staying with Darren would be better for him than staying with her. Darren was outgoing and flamboyant, and his personality would suit Jonathon's quiet caring nature.

"I have been thinking." Dorothy's announcement caught everyone's attention. "Maybe Chris could take his mum to the afternoon Tea Dances at the nursing home where I volunteer. They hold them twice a month. You should mention it to him, Gina. And she'll be welcome in our class too. We're such an easy-going, friendly group." She didn't add *now Basil's gone*, but it hung in the air for a few seconds. "You should definitely encourage Chris to come with his mum. He needs us, as much as Kathleen needs to dance."

"He could get all sensual, dancing with Gina." Darren's smile split his face again. His comic wink at her, the accompanying actions of his arms crossing the front of his body, with his hands caressing his shoulder and back while he swayed, made them all laugh.

All except Gina. She fought back the tears instead.

To change the subject she told them her idea about them taking their Allied Dancing Association medals. There were opportunities to work towards them twice a year.

Darren's eyes widened. "Dancing medals? I'd love to enter a competition, like you and Chris. Wouldn't you, Dorothy? We could be the talk of the North West dance circuit when we wow them with our sultry salidas and our shocking sacadas, not to mention our raunchy rulos."

"I told you not to mention our raunchy rulos, Darren." Dorothy playfully punched Darren in the arm as she made her joke.

"Joking aside, Dorothy, I fancy having a try at a competition. They must have one for the beginner or novice classes. I have the perfect 'Gothic type' song in mind as well. We'd have to dress the part. Dorothy, you'd have to wear black fishnet tights with holes in them and a red corset sort of top. I'd dress in black with a black cloak that has a red lining and maybe I'd have a pair of vampire teeth. Can you imagine the reaction?"

They laughed at the idea and started discussing the options and possibilities for their entry. As a group they imagined the choreography to the music as Darren hummed it, until it was almost midnight and Dorothy started yawning.

As the class got up to go home, Jonathon held back from the others and said quietly to Gina, "I've just remembered where I know that car from, the one with the teddies on the back shelf in Chris's drive. It belongs to Abbi. I used to work with her in a Southport nursing home, about five years ago. She's a carer."

Chapter Twenty-Three

On Saturday, true to form, Chris arrived on time to pick her up. The nerves tightening in her stomach weren't due to the competition. She'd been up since six that morning, washing and styling her hair, painting her nails to match her dress and putting on the minimal amount of make-up to stop her face from shining and looking too pale in the bright lights of the dance floor.

He opened the car boot to put her bag in, and laid her dress, in its protector bag, flat across the back shelf, letting it drape over the back seats.

"Everywhere locked?" he asked.

"Yes," she said. "I think I've brought much more than I need. I seem to have an awful lot of luggage for one dance."

"Let's hope we make it to the final, so it will be more than one dance." He held the door open for her to get in the car, and got in his own side, and started up the ignition. "I hope the rain stays off because I don't know how far we need to walk from the car park. I know we have to park at the back of the Floral Hall, but I'm not sure if we can get in that way, or if we have to walk around to the front doors." He glanced admiringly at her hair. "If the weather is really bad, I could drop you off at the front before I go and park."

Oh, please don't let us make stilted small talk all day, she thought, as they pulled out of her road. She was used to him driving in silence, but knowing that they'd fallen out and not rectified it before the trip made her feel awkward. She didn't want there to be an atmosphere between them.

"I'm—" He must have felt the same way as her, because they both spoke together.

"You go first," he said.

She wondered what he was going to say to her. Was she going to make a fool of herself with what she was about to say? She decided to say it anyway.

"I was nervous about seeing you today, and what your reactions would be after my outburst that night."

"So was I, but probably for different reasons."

She didn't realise she'd been holding her breath until she let out a sigh.

"I've wanted to apologise for laying into you before finding out the facts. I feel ashamed for jumping to conclusions. I tried to phone you to ask what was going on, but your number was always unavailable. I'm sorry."

"My fault. I suppose it should be me apologising for not telling you about my mum sooner. If you'd known, you wouldn't have thought I had another woman. I'm sorry too." He stopped talking to concentrate on negotiating a busy roundabout. "Although I'm not sure how you came to the assumption, when you saw a woman my mother's age – and she does look like a woman in her sixties from all angles – that she was my partner! I really don't have a penchant for older women."

She almost laughed. Had he really thought she'd been talking about his mum when they had their argument? He didn't seriously think she'd mistake his mum's rotund figure for a pregnancy, did he? So was he joking?

She glanced at him, but he didn't appear to be joking.

"Your mum's carer, what does she look like?"

"Look like? She's taller than you, bleached blonde hair, often tied back. Why do you ask?"

"Is she pregnant?"

"Yes, and it won't be long until she gives up work."

"The day after Valentine's Day I saw her car in your drive next to yours when I passed at six in the morning. Later, when I walked back home, your car wasn't there, but she came out of the house, got shopping out of the car and went back in. I didn't see your mum. I was under the impression you'd lost both parents. I thought—"

"So that was why you thought I was seeing someone else,

and believed it to be the reason I didn't go out with you on Valentine's evening?"

"Pretty much, yes."

He stayed silent until they passed through the busy traffic in Ainsdale, but it was not an awkward silence. He pulled into a garden centre car park.

"Come on, let's have a coffee here. We've enough time to stop, and this conversation is far too serious to have in the car."

He walked ahead of her, towards the cafe. Disappointment washed over her, when he didn't hold her hand or even walk at her side. Was he still annoyed with her?

"I feel a right fool," he said as he put the coffees on the table. "Despite all your accusations about me being with someone else and having a pregnant partner, I never for one moment suspected you were talking about Abbi. For some unearthly reason I thought you meant my mum. No wonder it didn't make sense."

"Why didn't you tell me about your mum sooner, or introduce us?" She couldn't understand why he could keep something so big – so important – from her. Her throat tightened, and a lump there threatened to stop her from breathing.

"It's difficult to explain."

"Try me. I had a gran, and I looked after her near the end. I suppose it's nothing like you and your mum, but she got muddled and forgetful and often frustrated and angry because she couldn't fend for herself and needed to rely on me. Other times, she thought she was holding me back from going out, or travelling, or moving away to work. She couldn't understand that I really did want to be with her."

"It's more than just being muddled and frustrated." He stared at his coffee as if he was lost for words, or finding it too painful. She wanted to reach out to him, but she still wasn't sure where they stood now. Where they back to being friends and nothing more?

"You're saying she has dementia or Alzheimer's? Didn't you trust me to understand?"

"I trust you implicitly. I don't tell people because I don't want it to become a circus. At the beginning, I told a few people and they kept turning up to help, except they weren't a help. They pitied me and tried to tell me what I should be doing for myself and what I should be doing for Mum. Most of their advice centred around putting her in a home, and, by doing that, allowing me to get on with my life. Were they well-meaning? Maybe, but I thought they were interfering. No way would I put Mum in a home. She was only just into her sixties, far too young to be sent to a place where she's always said she didn't want to end up."

"She was so young? How awful for you both. But why didn't you tell me this earlier, Chris? I know it isn't something you'd slip into a chat-up line, but we were getting on so well. At the risk of repeating myself, I would have understood."

"Mum has been going downhill for years. I think the shock of my father dying sparked it off. I've told the couple of girlfriends I've had in the past about Mum, and it was a disaster each time. Admittedly, they were nothing like you. I think they were only interested in the man in the uniform."

Gina felt the heat in her cheeks, remembering the thoughts she'd had when she saw him in his uniform. Fortunately, because he was playing with the froth in his mug with the spoon, he didn't appear to notice.

"Neither of them had your compassion, or caring nature, but they got sick of me calling off dates, or being late, or running home, because I had problems with Mum or the carer. I've been called a mummy's boy, told to cut the apron strings, put her in a home... Well, you can imagine the sort of thing, can't you?"

She could. Knowing that his dancing skills at the ball would earn him the nickname of Twinkle Toes, she could imagine the other, potentially harsher, names they might call him behind his back too.

"I know she only stayed a short time, but she liked the dance class, when you brought her. She could come along to that anytime, and you could join in and dance too."

"Yes, I know, but that's the thing. You know, the person you saw in that room isn't the Mum I grew up with, loved, relied on. Oh, I still love her, don't get me wrong, but the roles are reversed now. She is mostly child-like and she has tantrums. I'm her main carer and she relies on me. I pay for a private carer to sit with her when I go to work, or go out with you, or need a break. That's who I was phoning the day we made love. I needed to know that Abbi was okay to stay with Mum for a bit longer. How romantic is that, having to check with my mum's sitter if I can stay out late, and still be home before ten at night?"

He tried a smile, but it stopped at the corners of his mouth and he sighed.

"I fit my own life in around Mum and the hours the carer can work. I really wanted to go out with you on Valentine's evening, but the carer was out with her husband. I can't get anyone else in, because it takes a long time for Mum to settle in the house with a stranger. She's okay if I'm with her when we have company, but she can be demanding, as you saw at class. If she wants something, it always has to be that instant. It can be awkward, not to mention embarrassing, if the other person takes it personally. She can also be unpleasant quite suddenly, too, if the mood takes her. The Mum I grew up with was never unpleasant."

His eyes showed a watery glaze, but he blinked it away. She, on the other hand, wasn't so successful when the tears welled up in her eyes.

She waited for him to say something else, not trusting herself to speak without sounding self-pitying. Her thoughts were of sympathy for both of them, of course, but how long did he think he could keep from mentioning his mum to her, when they were going out, getting closer, talking of the future? How long was he intending to wait before deciding that they could be good enough together for her to become a part of his life with his mum?

As if reading her thoughts, he placed his hands on hers.

She had no control over the tears that escaped down her cheeks. She wanted to say that she wasn't crying because his mum took priority, and she wasn't even crying because he hadn't told her earlier. She understood his predicament, but she was crying for the life cut short of a woman in her prime, and the son who tried to do his best by her.

"I'm sorry, Gina. This probably isn't what you expected when we got together."

He squeezed her hands and waited until she looked at him.

"I wanted to introduce you to her. Who wouldn't? You're the girl my mother would've readily embraced into the family under normal circumstances. It's just that… Well, it takes her a while to accept change, to remember who people are on her good days, and not to feel threatened by them on her bad days, when her memory fails her. If they disappear from her life, it worries her, she gets anxious, and we have a terrible time getting her settled again."

He let go of her hands and checked his watch.

"We'd better get moving, we don't want to be late. You know, this competition means a lot to me. I was so proud of dancing with the most gorgeous girl at the ball. It was as if we'd been dancing together for years. I told Mum I'd been dancing again, and she was quite lucid talking about her dancing days and how she entered competitions with Dad. She couldn't remember if she'd danced in a competition with me. We hadn't, and I've never won a dancing prize in competitions or in classes. Even if we don't win something today, it will still be something I can talk about with her." He shrugged. "She'll no doubt forget our conversation, but for a short while she'll be proud of me entering. That's why I still wanted to do this competition today, even when we fell out. I thought, hoped, you would be professional about it and still go with me. I might not have seemed it at the time, but I was really happy when you agreed."

Back in the car, the talk moved away from his mum, and she told him all about the break-in and Jonathon. It surprised her that word hadn't got back to him at the station. He knew nothing about it, and apologised profusely until she had to stop him.

"You were away, and I know you aren't part of the investigating team, so there's no reason for them to tell you. I haven't heard anything more from the police after Mike Holmes stopped me. Maybe you could find out how the investigation is coming along and let me know, unofficially of course."

"I will do, and now tell me about your new job. I can't believe so much has happened in the few days I wasn't around. Does Paula know we're dancing in this competition?"

"Yes, she does. She knew before I told her because she'd seen our names on the list, and she said," Gina made little quotation marks with her fingers, "'Well, you should be in with a chance now that Karl and I can't dance in it.' Apparently they enter each year and are more often than not in the final six. He runs a dance school in Bolton, and his wife and her dance partner enter and win professional competitions in the Argentine tango section."

"You'd think they'd dance together, being married, wouldn't you?"

"It's often like that in the dance world. Just because you're a couple doesn't mean you have the same taste or skill in the same dances. A lot of men prefer the ballroom to latin as they don't have the supple movements in their hips for latin. Or it can be something as simple as their differing tastes in music which decides the dances they prefer."

She told him about Darren's ambition to enter a competition with Dorothy as soon as they perfected their routine. He laughed, making the creases at the corner of his eyes deepen, and his shoulders visibly dropped into a relaxed position.

"Well, watch out, Karl's wife and dance partner! An odd couple from the Gina Pendleton School of Dance have their eyes firmly set on your trophy." He glanced at Gina, before looking back at the road as he said, "And with your skills to help them, I don't think that's as far-fetched as it sounds."

He drove on to the road along the front of the Marine Lake, passed the hotels and continued towards The Floral Hall. Because there was a break in the rain, he turned into the carpark.

"Well, Gina, we've arrived. Are you ready to help me show them what we're capable of?"

Chapter Twenty-Four

The interior of the Floral Hall was nothing like the Blackpool Tower Ballroom. Gina had been to the Tower Ballroom, in her own competitions as a teenager, and it had appeared so grand to her then that it had made a lasting impression on her. Here there were no plush velvet seats and ornate gold painted carvings around the walls, nor was there a balcony or a famous rise-and-fall theatre organ. A little part of her was disappointed that their first competition together should be in a building that, although modern and bright with a purpose-built floor, was lacking in grandeur and history. She tried to push the thought out of her mind that if things didn't go well, it could be her last competition with Chris too.

They registered at the door as they went in, and got their number. There were fifteen registered for the Sequence Ballroom category and they were number twelve. The other two categories, Latin and Classical, had fewer entries, and were judged separately. Chris confessed to her that he'd hoped there wouldn't be as many as there were, so if they were the first to be eliminated it wouldn't seem so bad.

She laughed. "You forget, we've only been dancing together since the ball, whereas some of these couples will have been dancing together for years. At least we're here, and giving them someone to compete against."

He rested his arm across her shoulders and guided her through the next set of double doors.

"True. I guess I'm putting more pressure on myself than I need to. Let's just go and have some fun. I'm going to get changed so I'll meet you back here in a few minutes."

Gina changed into her dress. It had crossed her mind that it might be rather too elaborate a dress for the event, but she had a wardrobe full of cocktail dresses for dancing, and hadn't been able to wear them to a dance, since several years before her gran died.

The one she'd chosen for the competition had been a favourite of her gran's. It was a rich turquoise silk with a skirt consisting of six full layers of chiffon over the silk. The top had a fitted beaded bodice, and a wide band of lace in the same colour as the silk ran front and back and fitted over her shoulders.

She and Gran had been on a trip to the theatre in London and had arrived too early for the theatre opening its doors. The road that ran down the side of the theatre was Drury Lane, and it was full of shops selling dancing shoes and dresses. They'd spotted the dress on a display model in the side window and both of them loved it instantly. The sign on it announced it was reduced, and the price tag showed such a vast reduction that her gran had walked into the shop and asked what size the dress was, before Gina had reluctantly turned away from looking at it through the window. It was Gina's size and the only one left. There were a few tiny holes in the chiffon at the side, where it had caught on something, and the zip was faulty. After seeing it on Gina, her gran had managed to get the assistant to deduct even more, to cover the cost of repairs by a seamstress, although Gran had repaired it herself by adding beading over the holes.

The reaction from Chris would have been worth triple the price of the dress. His mouth dropped open and the admiration in his eyes shone from where he'd stopped in his tracks, fifteen to twenty yards away.

"Do you like it?" She gave him a twirl and the skirt floated around in a circle, settling into place with a slight bounce as she stopped.

"Stop fishing for compliments." His gaze took in her full height from her cream satin shoes to the beaded combs in her hair. "You know you look good."

"Just good?" She gave him a mischievous smile and laughed. "I know it suits me, but it doesn't harm to tell me too."

"You look stunning, but then you always do, with or without the dress." He gently held her chin and tilted it to make her lips meet his. He kissed her, slowly at first, building up to such an urgency that it took Gina by surprise. She responded, but just as she wondered if they were indeed back on to their original footing in their relationship, he stopped abruptly. She looked in his eyes for an answer, but found none there.

"Right. Talk me through what happens next." He'd changed the subject and his body language said *We've moved on; don't dissect the kiss*. She could do nothing but explain the competition to him.

"Each section is judged separately, and it looks as though the ballroom group is up first. Each couple demonstrates their sequence choreography alone on the floor, unlike other sequence competitions, where, if they were all being judged on their Rumba 1 for example, they'd all be on the floor together and eliminated one by one until only the top three remain. It's because we've all choreographed our own dances and the judges need to concentrate on them fully. Only the top six go through to the next round. They dance it one couple at a time again. This time only one winner is chosen."

"Okay." He looked around the room. "I thought there'd be more people watching than this. If we're going to be dancing on our own in front of the judges, I'm glad it's not a packed hall."

The music started and a few couples walked on to the floor to dance. She suggested they dance, too, as a warm-up, so they joined the small group for the waltz to the song *Are You Lonesome Tonight?* She relaxed into his arms, wishing the lighting wasn't so bright.

They continued dancing until they announced the call for the entrants for Ballroom Sequence. Chris's palms were clammy as they held hands to walk over to the group by the judges table.

"Are you nervous?"

He nodded, and she was surprised. She thought as a policeman he must have been in all sorts of nerve-wracking situations, and dancing in a competition was the least dangerous of all of them. When she said that to him, he laughed.

"It's more because I might make a fool of myself and I don't want to let you down. I'll be fine once we're on the floor, I promise."

They watched the couples dancing their inventive choreographed sequence dances, every now and then making quiet little comments like "Interesting manoeuvre" or "Neat!" None of the other couples had picked a foxtrot to choreograph. There were two Viennese waltzes, three waltzes, four quicksteps and five tangos. Gina secretly hoped it that being the only foxtrot was a good omen.

Their turn soon arrived. They walked on to the dance floor, as the announcer gave their details:

"Next up we have Gina Pendleton, a freelance dance teacher from Paula's School of Dance, and Christopher Jackson, an officer in the Merseyside Police. They dance a sequence foxtrot called the Freshby Foxtrot."

They adopted the closed position dance hold and waited. The music didn't play, and Gina began to fear there was something wrong with the CD. Just when she felt Chris tense as if to break the hold and investigate, the first bar of the introduction played over the speakers.

She counted the beat through the smile she'd held waiting for the music to start. One, two, three, four...

"Now!" she said without moving her lips, as the Tony Evans band crooned the first line of *The Way You Make Me Feel*.

The two minutes they were allowed passed so quickly that she almost felt cheated when the music was stopped. They moved to the side to make way for the next couple.

"I can't believe how fast the time went," whispered Chris. "How do you think we did?"

She was still on a high when she answered. "I honestly think we danced our best sequence yet."

He took hold of her hand, which she'd left hanging relaxed by her thigh, and squeezed it. He didn't let go of it and they were still holding hands as the last couple finished dancing.

They were told to sit down while the judges discussed who to choose as the finalists, so Chris released her hand and put his arm around her shoulders instead, as he ushered her back to their table.

"Who would you put your money on to win?"

She giggled and told him she now imagined a row of bookmakers, standing beside their electric boards, showing the odds for each couple.

"I'm glad they don't allow the bookies in, it could be disheartening. Do you think we have a chance?"

"It's just my opinion, but I think *The Tilly Tango* is a winner, but it will be a close call. The other contenders could be *The Vespa Quickstep* and *The Winslatter Waltz*. It depends what the judges are looking for, of course."

"Not us then? I think I'd place us in the top two."

"You can't vote for your own, that would be cheating."

He was about to reply, when the man with the microphone asked if he could have the following finalists to line up at the front. He read out the numbers of the six pairs.

"Number twelve, Gina. That's us! Wow, we're in the final!" Chris stood and offered her his arm to link, as they made their way to the row of dancers gathering at the front of the stage. She couldn't control the smile on her face. Although she thought it their best performance, she didn't think they would get into the finals. She was happy for Chris, knowing this was something Kathleen would love to hear all about.

They were the last couple to dance. The longer they had to wait, the more she could feel Chris tremble. Twice she had to whisper to him to relax.

Their names were called, and he led her on to the floor.

For the second time, they waited in foxtrot hold for the music to start. This time the introduction began straight away.

She was going through the dance in her head: *slow, quick, quick, progressive chasse, slow, quick, quick...* Did Chris hesitate on that step? She stopped going through it in her mind and let her feet do it automatically. She felt sure Chris had shuffled slightly to catch up after his slight hesitation. The music stopped, and their time was called.

They stood with the other couples, each wishing the other good luck, and then walked back to their tables to wait for the results.

"Sorry, Gina, I made a mistake. For a moment there, my mind went blank, even though I knew the dance inside out. I forgot the next step and had to catch up."

"Don't worry about it. It's all experience, we can practise more, and be well prepared for the next competition," she said, hoping he wouldn't say this one was their last. "Besides, it was an achievement to be amongst the finalists."

He didn't contradict her.

The man with the microphone stood up and began to speak. "I'd like to announce the result of today's final in the Ballroom Sequence dance category. The winning dance is *The Tilly Tango*, arranged by Helen and Hugh Borwich."

The couple bowed and curtsied and received their bouquet and a shield to a round of applause.

"Well done. You said that would be the winner." Chris smiled at her and reached out, as if to put his arm round her, but stopped as a familiar voice spoke from behind.

"You messed up," Paula said to him. "I'd have had you in my top two, until you forgot your step at the open impetus turn."

Next she addressed herself to Gina. "A bit presumptuous of you to say you taught at my school in your intro, considering you're still in your probationary period. In the end though, with a performance like that, it could work in my favour. I'm putting together a team for a competition in the summer. Let me know if you both want to be a part of it." She didn't wait for a reply, but added, "Sooner, rather than later," before hobbling off on her crutches to speak with the organisers.

"Some might say that compliment was better than winning." Chris was smiling. "I think you've added another admirer to your list."

"Another?"

"You're doing it again, fishing for compliments!" He gave her a cheeky smile. "But you do look even more beautiful today, and I'm proud to be your dance partner." He leant forward and kissed her lips before saying, "Come on, let's dance a little before the next section of judging starts."

They danced close together to the music, and she didn't care that they didn't have the correct hold, or that they shuffled, more than danced. At one point she tucked her head into his chest and as he kissed the top of her head she could feel his warm breath on her fringe.

When the music stopped, they agreed that there wasn't any point in staying at the event, so they both went to get changed back into their day clothes, and arranged to meet at the door to the car park.

In the car, Gina played over in her mind the effects Chris's kisses had on her. Never before had she been so sure that the man she was sitting next to was the one she wanted to spend the rest of her life with.

His voice broke into her thoughts.

"We've come together at the wrong time, Gina. If we'd met before Mum's onset of dementia, it would have been better, even if it wasn't ideal. Trouble is, I can't foresee a right time, and I'm not sure I want to, because that means Mum would be..." There was a catch in his voice and he stopped, unable to continue.

Despite her own shock and dismay at his words, her first thought was his dilemma, needing to meet the demands of his mum and put them over his own needs. She reached over to put her hand on his. It stayed there for the rest of the journey back to her house.

He got her bag and dress out of the car and carried them to the door for her. As she opened the door he said, "Can I come in?"

"Of course you can."

He looked serious and her heart sank. Obviously he wanted to talk. Out of habit she went through to the kitchen to put the kettle on, and then sat next to him on her sofa.

He took a deep breath. "It's been a funny sort of day. I left home thinking that, at best, we could still be friends. I'm glad we ironed out a huge misunderstanding, but it's left me even more confused. I'm sorry about making the mistake in the dance, but I let my mind stray. I was thinking about more important things than entering a dancing competition just to make an impression on my mum. That will result in a fifteen-minute conversation which she'll have forgotten by the end of the day." He ran his fingers through the front of his hair, making it even more tousled than usual. "I was thinking about us. You and me, and our future, if we have one together."

A lump rose in her throat, but she swallowed it down and managed to speak in a steady voice.

"Would it help if I told you I love you? Because I do. It is the only thing I know for certain in a year that started with so many upsets and questions."

He wrapped his arms around her shoulders and pulled her towards him. He was wearing the lemon and patchouli aftershave which teased her senses, and his chest radiated the warmth she needed, in a room that held a chill in the air comparable to the one crowding her chest. She waited for his answer.

He took another deep breath and held it. She felt and heard the rhythmic beat of his heart, whilst she felt sure hers had stopped, still waiting for his reply. Eventually he let the breath out in one long, resigned, drawn-out exhalation.

"I love you too."

She relaxed a little. Her heart hadn't stopped. The tension started to flow out of her, only to stall at his next words.

"I do love you, but I can't offer you the full stability of a proper relationship. I don't even know why I got us into this mess, except that – that first moment I saw you, my heart controlled my head. I couldn't settle. I was thinking of you all the time."

"Then we can adapt, work around your mum and your shifts, and—"

He kissed her softly on the lips, not with passion, but with genuine warmth.

"I love you so much, Gina Pendleton. I don't want anyone else, just you. Which was why I drove miles from Scotland to see you that night. I don't want to lose you, but I can't ask you to wait around indefinitely."

The lump in her throat returned, and a cascade of tears escaped and ran down her cheeks. She wiped her eyes with the back of her hand, while she delved in her pocket for a tissue. She shook her head with despair. How could she convince him that she wouldn't ask more of him than he was able to fulfil in between caring for his mum? It seemed he could only see the black and white in the situation, nothing in between.

He hugged her tightly, so suddenly that it knocked the tissue out of her hand and she had to use her sleeve to wipe her eyes. If he noticed, he didn't say, but she rummaged in her pocket again and found another.

"Abbi will be on maternity leave soon, and Mum will have to get used to someone else coming in and caring for her. We will have our work cut out settling her. That means I'll have to be around her a lot more, with no spare time for much else." His fingers played with the ends of her hair as he went on. "I've had a lot of trouble at home these past two weeks. With me being away overnight twice in such a short time, Mum became extremely agitated even though she is mostly happy with Abbi. At one point I had to take her to the hospital to have her checked, because I thought she was having a seizure. It's made me think about her reaction to the next change in her life. I'm going to contact the agency this week to see if they have a carer Mum will accept, and then let them visit gradually over the coming months, building up until they can step into Abbi's position permanently. It will be costly, but it's the easiest way for Mum and for everyone else around her. I'm not sure I can offer a relationship with anyone, if Mum is going to be upset every time there is change in her life. It's traumatic for all concerned, not just her."

He released his hold on her shoulders and turned her to face him. She could see his eyes were watery, but he had much better control over his tears than she had.

With the softest of touches he wiped the last of her tears away from her cheeks and gazed at her, as if taking everything in, saving it to memory, one last time.

"Now, I don't know where we go from here. I may not be able to see you much over the next few months. I'll be busy once I've arranged someone to cover Abbi's maternity leave, and then there'll be a period of uncertainty and maybe trying a few carers."

"I'll wait, Chris." Her voice came out as barely a whisper. "Please, don't give up on us."

He suddenly stood up, and bent forward, his hand shaking as he lifted her chin to place the lightest of kisses on her mouth. Then, leaving her sitting on the sofa, he turned away and strode down the hall.

"See you soon. I'll call you."

She whispered, "See you soon?"

The front door closed and she was left alone.

Chapter Twenty-Five

Gina sat still, gazing at the door, wondering what had just happened. Were they still in a relationship or not? His leaving had been so sudden, she hadn't had any time to collect her thoughts and stall him or to get answers to her questions. Her lip quivered, and to stop a possible repeat of useless tears, she headed for the kitchen and switched the kettle back on.

While she was waiting for it to boil, she yanked the beaded slide out of her hair, pulled out all the hair grips, un-twirled the sides and shook her hair free. She tore off a few sheets of kitchen towel and after wetting them under the tap, rubbed them roughly all over her face to remove the make-up. She did the same with a few more sheets, until her face was clean. She hated wearing make-up, and the fresh feel to her clean face was a relief. If only scrubbing away at everything else going on in her life could make her feel so good.

She was halfway through her coffee and chocolate biscuit when she knew she had to talk to him again. They'd already had a few misunderstandings, and this one had to be settled before it grew out of all proportion.

The rain from the morning had returned, and she pulled her hood over her head, realising as she did so that she'd forgotten to brush her hair after pulling it out of its style. Still, the way the rain ran down her hood and settled on her shoulders, she was going to arrive at his house looking dishevelled anyway.

As his house came into her sight it was apparent that his car wasn't in the drive, nor was Abbi's car. Had he gone somewhere else after leaving hers and not arrived home yet, or had he been home and taken Kathleen out with him? There was only one way to find out.

She rang the doorbell and hoped he hadn't left Kathleen in

the house on her own, or she'd be alarmed seeing a stranger at the door. Nobody answered, so Gina did something she hated other people doing, and peered in through the window. The room was bigger than she expected from the front of the house. It was tidy, with no ornaments and sparsely furnished, and the door from the room to the rest of the house was shut. There was no sign of life in the room, for which she was grateful, because had she scared Kathleen by being a sudden face at the window, she would never have forgiven herself.

She stood at the front door for a moment, at a loss as to what to do next. She hadn't planned further than talking to him face to face on the doorstep, so that Kathleen wouldn't see her. She could carry on walking to the Pine Woods and try knocking again on the way back.

The rain had worked its way through the top canopy of trees and was forming puddles on the carpet of pine needles under foot. She avoided the deeper puddles but walked through the shallow ones. A couple ahead of her with two small children were taking great delight in jumping in the deeper puddles, but they had been sensible and come prepared with knee-high wellies and knee-length waterproofs.

She heard a rustle to the side and stopped to watch a red squirrel scurry along a branch, jump to the next tree and scale the trunk until it was out of sight. The cries of the children grew fainter, so she walked slowly to allow them to get further ahead and leave her with the peace and the bird song. The smell of the pine trees competed with the musty smell of the woodland floor, but she loved the smell of both, and breathed in deeply in the hope that it would keep her calm and settle her thoughts.

Large droplets of rain water dripped on to the front of her hood and down her face. If she felt the urge to cry again, now was the time to do it, when it wouldn't be noticeable, but typically she seemed to be all cried out.

When she reached the car park where she and Chris had practised their foxtrot, she danced a promenade, followed by a feather step, leading into a curving three step, not caring if anyone was watching. After the last promenade, she carried on walking down the road to the hut at the beginning of the Pine Woods trail.

She checked the time, and saw she'd been walking for an hour. If Chris's car wasn't back in his drive, she'd carry on walking home.

"Well?"

She knew what Shelley meant, but wasn't going to give her the answer straight away. She'd only nipped into the shop for milk.

"Well, what?"

"Did you win the competition? Did you kiss and make up? Do you have anything else to tell me, while there's no one in the shop?"

"We didn't win, but we got in the final six, so that was a pleasant surprise." She put her milk down on the counter.

"And…?"

"And it's complicated."

"If it was straightforward, you wouldn't have gossip for me. Give me it in a nutshell, and if I don't understand, I'll nip around to yours later and you can tell me it all, while Geoff minds the shop."

Geoff made faces behind Shelley's back, and without turning around she said to him, "And you can stop making those faces!"

Gina gave her a quick outline, without mentioning Chris's mum, which was difficult. She could see that Shelley suspected there was more that she'd left out, but it wasn't up to her to tell her friends something he'd obviously never mentioned to Geoff.

"Do you want Geoff to have a word with him?"

"Oi! Keep me out of it. Sorry, Gina, love, but men don't go asking each other personal things, and giving advice like that. It's a bit… well, intrusive, and, you know… soppy like."

"I wouldn't want you to have a word, Geoff. If you want to pop around later," she added to Shelley, "you'll be welcome – but that doesn't mean I'll tell you everything. I'm not even sure it's alright for me to tell you anything."

"It sounds cryptic enough to stir my interest. I'll be around later."

Later, Shelley swore she wouldn't tell if Gina confided in her. "What we talk about here, stays here," she promised, as she opened the wine and shook the crisps into a bowl.

After some hesitation, Gina told her the bits she needed to know about Chris's mum and her carer, without going into all of it in minute detail. Every now and then she stopped to remind Shelley not to repeat it to anyone.

She'd almost reached the part where Chris dropped her at home, when there was a knock at the door. She opened it to see Darren and Dorothy standing there.

As Gina introduced them to Shelley, she brought in two more glasses and placed them on the coffee table. Darren had brought a few bottles of lager and Shelley poured Dorothy a wine. They'd been texting each other to see if either had heard how she and Chris had got on at the competition. Dorothy had spied Chris with Kathleen at the nursing home where she volunteered with the Age Concern charity, and was going to ask him about the competition results.

"I tried to find a break in the conversation I was having with an elderly gent, but by the time he stopped his tale, they'd gone out of reception. And the receptionist wouldn't tell me what it was they were talking about. I hope they were asking about the tea dances. I'm sure Kathleen would enjoy them."

"Maybe she enjoyed listening to his account of our morning's dancing, and wanted to join a group herself." Gina hoped that he hadn't gone along to see if they had any vacant rooms for her. If he was thinking of sending Kathleen to a nursing home because he felt under pressure from her, she'd be mortified.

When Shelley, without thinking, voiced the same thoughts, Darren and Dorothy turned towards Gina for an explanation. Shelley mouthed 'Sorry' and looked full of remorse for her mistake. Gina decided a twist on the truth would only be a small white lie.

"Kathleen's carer is having a baby," she explained to them. "Chris is looking for care for her while Abbi is on maternity leave, but I'm sure his intention isn't for her to stay in a nursing home permanently."

Shelley tried to redeem herself by changing the subject to Darren and Dorothy's Argentine tango progress.

"Go on then, give me a demonstration. In fact I'd like to try a little bit myself."

Dorothy giggled, but looked pleased and willing to put on their show. Gina turned the lights on in the dance room and plugged in the speakers. She found herself surprised that the pair had improved so much in a week. Shelley was impressed, and begged to borrow Darren to try out some of the basic steps. After the four of them had swapped partners and danced though a few songs, Dorothy announced that it was nearly time for her to go home. Shelley looked at her watch.

"I didn't realise it was that late. I'll have to go, too. I promised Geoff I'd do his early start tomorrow." She grabbed her coat and bag, and as she gave Gina a hug at the front door, she said quietly into her ear, "Sorry about my big mouth, blurting things out before my brain is in gear. I hope it hasn't made things awkward." In a loud voice she said, "Bye you two, thanks for the company and dancing."

Gina tried texting Chris the next day, but got no reply. She didn't hear anything from him until four days later, when he turned up at her door in his uniform. He was still on his shift, so he turned down her offer of sitting down with a drink, and instead stayed in the hall to talk to her.

"Sorry I haven't been in touch before now," he said, and without explaining any reason for that, he launched into his reason for calling on her. "I found out some of news for you at the station today, about the reason for Lucy's involvement in the break-ins and her connection to the guy we arrested."

"So there was a connection?" She couldn't comprehend why Lucy should know the drug user, since they had absolutely nothing in common.

"It seems that once you chucked Tony out, he decided he didn't want to stay with Lucy after all. She felt humiliated, and had always hated you for being the one he cared about when she was dating him. Apparently he told her it was only fun to be with her because she was the 'bit on the side' as he called it, and it seems he'd lost interest when he was left with her as a 'proper' girlfriend. He moved out after only two nights in her house, and found himself another girlfriend to live with."

"So he didn't stay with her? I thought she was the girlfriend he mentioned in his alibi. I suppose I presumed he wanted to be with her."

"No, far from it. Anyway, she came across the group of layabouts by the railway path near the woods to the dunes. When they asked her for money, it gave her an idea and she told them they could earn it. So she paid the drug addict to set you up and frighten you a little. She kept hold of Tony's spare car key which you'd sent back to him at her place, thinking he might as well be implicated too. In other words, she'd be getting revenge on both of you at the same time. But the guy messed up the first time he broke into the dance school, and didn't plant any evidence to implicate you. Of course neither of them knew that your alibi that night would be a room full of police officers at the ball."

They both laughed at the irony of it.

"Then the guy became greedy. He's admitted he started to blackmail her into giving him more and more money. I think she was relieved when she was eventually found out. She was frightened by him, and she was running out of money."

"How did he know where I lived? And how did he get hold of my watch?"

"She dropped him off at your place one night in Tony's car, and told him where to find your watch because she'd noticed it one night when she'd been in your bedroom with Tony. He sneaked in and pinched it during your dance class when the door was left open. Remember how easy it was for me to walk in with my mum that time?"

"She'd been through all my things while I was at work? How dare she!" Gina was sickened and embarrassed by how easily she'd been taken for a fool by both Tony and Lucy.

"He also got the car key from her and was using Tony's car as a getaway when he went out 'on the rob' with his mates. It seems Tony didn't even notice his petrol going down so much, and there must have been a rancid smell in the car after they'd used it."

"I find it difficult to believe that I ever thought Lucy was my friend. Yet she didn't show any of these nasty traits when we hung out together."

"Don't go giving her a good character reference, will you? She could have caused you serious harm. I've heard all about you being choked, from the officers concerned. I realise now how much you played it down when you told me. She will be charged, although the courts may be lenient because of the blackmail issue."

His radio crackled and he looked towards the squad car. Terry was beckoning to him.

"Have to go, we must have had a call come through." He was half way down the path when he waved and shouted, "I'll call you."

She imagined he would wait several more days before he got in touch, but so long as he kept his word and stayed in touch, she would wait.

The news he'd delivered was too good to keep to herself, and she knew Shelley would enjoy listening to that snippet of gossip, so she phoned the shop to see if Shelley wanted to meet up that evening. Her plans of a girly night with wine were scuppered when Shelley told her she couldn't go out, but suggested Gina joined her at the shop for a cuppa instead. They sat in the back room going over all the information that Chris had given her, with Geoff standing by the door trying to listen. He was keeping watch on the shop at the same time, and they had to keep repeating the parts he'd missed when he dashed off to serve a customer.

When there was a lull in the conversation, Geoff broke the silence.

"You know, Gina, Chris is a good man, and the pair of you belong together. Anyone can see that. I'm not into talking of love and all that soppy stuff, but I really hope it works out for you both in the end."

She smiled at him. "I've been doing a lot of thinking since

Chris introduced me to his mum. He is so caring and unselfish, putting his mum's needs before his own, comforting me when I was upset over the vandals. He even sorted out my debts that were caused by Tony. Looking back, I wonder what I ever saw in Tony beyond his good looks. He was so shallow and selfish. He never put me first, and everything revolved around him. I can see why he picked me; I was an easy target." She sighed. "I missed looking after my gran and having someone around the house. I suppose I was flattered by his attentions. He did me a favour on Boxing Day. He brought me to my senses." She looked at Shelley who was nodding in agreement. "Are you going to say *I told you so*?"

"I wouldn't dream of it."

"You're lucky, girl. She says it to me all the time." Geoff ducked out of the way of a cushion thrown by Shelley and retreated into the shop.

As Gina was leaving to go home, Geoff surprised her with a box of hot chocolate pods for her coffee maker, and a bunch of daffodils and freesias. She was so touched by his generosity, she gave him a genuine tight hug and a kiss on the cheek.

He blushed. "Aw, girl, you'll have them all queuing to give me a hug and kiss in exchange for a few flowers. Not that I'd mind, but I think you've had such a rough time lately, you deserve them."

"You big soft lump." Shelley put her arm around Geoff's shoulders, and grinned at Gina. "He's right, though. You make yourself a nice hot chocolate at bedtime, and have these marshmallows and chocolate flakes to top it."

She was attempting to drink the last drop from the large mug of hot chocolate, tipping her head right back to catch the part-melted flake and marshmallows, when she heard a knock.

Chris was standing at the front door. She stepped aside to let him in, but he stopped in front of her.

"You have, erm – something on your nose, here." He pointed to his own nose.

She rubbed her fingers across her nose and tilted it up for his inspection. He laughed and shook his head. Gently using his index finger, he wiped the chocolate from her nose, showed her his finger to prove he'd rescued her, and kissed the top of her head.

She felt lightheaded, and tingles of excitement wove their way up her spine. This promised to be a relaxed call, despite him still being in his uniform. He led the way through to the sofas and when they were sitting side by side, he spoke first.

"I can't begin to tell you how much I've thought about you, since you said on Saturday that you loved me. The whole Lucy and Tony thing had me thinking, too. I thought that Tony must be mad to two-time you, and then give you up without a fight once he was discovered. I found myself wondering why he gave up so easily, and then I realised that in some way I was doing the same. I was giving up on us, letting you slip away, and I was mad to do it because you were all I wanted. Then Darren handed me a lifeline. Somehow he knew I was looking for a carer—"

"That was Shelley. Sorry, she let it slip, when we were all having drinks here."

He placed a finger gently on her lips.

"I guessed it would be something along those lines." He smiled. "As it turned out Shelley did me a big favour. Darren suggested Jonathon would be an ideal carer, after seeing how he got on so well with my mum at your class. So I got in touch with Jonathon, and he's been around a few times, and sat with Mum, I even found them, dancing, actually dancing, in the living room. I've had a chat with Abbi, too. She doesn't think she'll go back to working such long hours after she's had the baby, especially with her partner on shift work as well. So I've offered the job to Jonathon full-time, from the day Abbi leaves us. He's going to move in permanently, and I'll buy him a car to take Mum out and about."

"That's wonderful news!"

"Isn't it? When the time is right, I can gradually stay away for longer periods, and I can stay here overnight more often after shifts, and still get home in time for Mum waking in the morning, if need be. Then, at a natural time for me to move out and leave the two of them living there alone, I can just pop in and out to visit. If Jonathon can live there long-term, as he hopes to, and Mum copes well with it, you and I will be able to live together."

He pulled her in towards him as he went on, "Do you want to carry this conversation on upstairs? Because I can stay overnight." His lips twitched at the corner. "I've put an overnight bag in the car just in case."

"What about your mum?"

"Jonathon called around, and told me to get over here. He thinks it's time I committed myself to our relationship, and of course he's right. He's staying overnight with Mum, so we have a whole night to ourselves. Is that okay with you, Miss Pendleton?"

She laughed. "It certainly is, Mr Jackson, but first you need to get out of that uniform. It's the man underneath that I'm interested in, not the clothes."

"That's what I like to hear."

He bent his head down to hers, and as soon as his fingers touched her chin she lifted her head for the kiss she'd desired for so long. His lips met hers and the warmth of his mouth sent a hot current running up and down her spine. All her nerve endings tingled as she pressed herself closer to his body. Putting one hand in the small of his back and the other around his neck, she drew him in closer still. His breath tasted of fresh mint, and his patchouli aftershave teased her senses. She could feel his desire building and hers responded to it. She wanted to be so close to him that she practically wore his skin, wanted to feel his pleasure pulse with hers, and then feel secure with his arms around her and his breath on her face as he slept afterwards.

Just as her longing became unbearable, he released her, took her by the hand and led her up the stairs.

"Let's get this uniform off then."

THE END

Fantastic Books
Great Authors

Meet our authors and discover our exciting range:

- Gripping Thrillers
- Cosy Mysteries
- Romantic Chick-Lit
- Fascinating Historicals
- Exciting Fantasy
- Young Adult and Children's Adventures
- Non-Fiction

Visit us at:
www.crookedcatbooks.com

Join us on facebook:
www.facebook.com/crookedcatbooks

Printed in Great Britain
by Amazon